NORTHLAND

NORTHLAND

CARA DEE

Northland

Copyright © 2015 by Cara Dee

All rights reserved

Edited by Silently Correcting Your Grammar, LLC.
Formatted by Rachel Lawrence.

DEDICATION

Dedication missing because Cara dropped her laptop in the snow.

CHAPTER 1

Opening the shed behind the house, Kyle rummaged through his stores of food and selected dinners for the next week to be brought inside. Wolf, his two-year-old Husky, barked and wagged his tail, reminding Kyle of his presence—as if Kyle would forget.

"You hungry?" Kyle grinned behind his face mask at his gray-and-white-coated companion, then located a treat from today's catch that was only half-frozen. "Savor it." He tossed the fish to Wolf, who started gnawing and chewing happily. "No food tomorrow." He was flying down to Nome with Wolf then, and the pup tended to get sick. Less food helped on travel days. "You need to fatten up a bit if you're gonna survive outside." Wolf was miserable in the house and only lived indoors when it hit forty below.

With his selection of caribou, whale, and fish in his arms, Kyle headed back inside the small house he shared with his father and ten-year-old niece and stripped down to camos and his hoodie.

As he stuffed the freezer and fridge with food, he listened to his dad talk about the weather. Lately, it was all the man did. This time there was a traffic warning for ice fog. Common enough.

"That's fascinating, Dad. Soon you'll tell me it's gonna snow,

1

too." The new year had just started, which meant his hometown was covered in snow and blanketed in constant darkness. It'd be weeks before Barrow saw the sun again.

"You giving your old man attitude?" his dad muttered gruffly from the living room.

"Every day," Kyle agreed. "Where's Lani? I thought we could get tacos. Oh, I stocked the kitchen, by the way. You're set for a week, and then Roger will drop by when the water tank gets refilled. He'll take out the honey bucket too, and help you with firewood."

Dad snorted and ignored the last part of what Kyle had said. "If you think you can bribe that girl with Taco Tuesday, you don't know her very well. She can hold a grudge. Takes after your brother—God rest his soul."

Kyle sighed. It was like this every time he took off for work outside of Barrow. Lani would ask to come with him, he'd say no, she'd get pissed.

Just then, both men heard a vicious shriek from Lani's room. "You can take your stupid tacos and shove 'em, Uncle Kyle!"

Kyle winced.

"Don't let her talk to you that way, son," Dad told him. "I won't be around forever, you know. Some day you'll be her guardian."

"Stop being so fucking morbid. You broke your hip. You're not dying." Kyle shook his head and walked to Lani's room. Dad was still right. Kyle had to talk to Lani about her tantrums. It had been five years now since Kyle's brother and sister-in-law had died, and Lani had exchanged grief for guilt cards and excuses a long time ago.

"I'm coming in." Kyle knocked on Lani's door before opening it. He found her lying on her stomach on her bed, face pressed into her pillow. "What have we said about being polite in this house, Ilannaq?"

Using her full name usually got her attention.

"That it's overrated?" she quipped sullenly.

There was a reason Kyle was uncomfortable and didn't like kids. He adored his niece—loved her beyond words, really—but he

2

wasn't cut out to be a parent.

"Try again." Kyle sat down on the edge of her bed and rolled her over, only to see her eyes filled with both tears and venom. "Looks can't kill, so quit it. Why're you crying?"

It was only a matter of time before Kyle's façade broke. Lani had the same black hair and silvery eye color as the rest of the Shaw men. But unlike their fair skin and Caucasian looks, Lani had inherited her mother's beautiful Inupiat features. It was her expressive eyes that were her biggest weapons when she wanted something.

Her bottom lip trembled, and she looked away dramatically. "I'm just gonna be so alone, Uncle Kyle." *Sniffle, sniffle.* "I'll be up here with Gramps in the darkness...no Wolf, either...while you're working at an exciting adventure retreat with your friends."

Talk about glorifying the coming three months.

Kyle was looking forward to going back to the O'Connor Adventure Retreat. It had become one of his favorite places in Alaska because there was always something to do. Plenty of rivers nearby for fishing, lots of wildlife, work, and good company.

The Retreat was pure luxury, too. Everything from solar panels and generators to firewood and battery packs kept the place running. It had in-fucking-door plumbing, a swimming pool, bathrooms with heated floors, a barbecue area, sauna and steam room, and other amenities Kyle never took for granted.

He worked all over Alaska, but the Retreat near the Bering Land Bridge Preserve took the prize. Surrounded by a miniscule, man-made forest, the O'Connors hosted backpackers in a large, two-story cabin with bunk beds, shower room, kitchen, and common room. In the three-story lodge across the yard, the staff lived comfortably in their own bedrooms and shared bathrooms and kitchen. Then in the third building, which faced the yard in the middle, they ran a bed-and-breakfast for those who had more dough than backpackers. There was also a restaurant, bar, a fucking spa, the indoor swimming pool, and a wraparound porch on the two first floors. And in the past two years, they'd added ten small cabins to accommodate the rich folk who wanted more privacy.

It was crazy.

The guests flying in from the Lower 48 probably didn't know how luxurious it was, what with the weather conditions and remoteness making everything so much harder in Alaska.

All that said, though? It was hard work. To maintain those high standards, the O'Connors were constantly expanding, and everything had to be done both perfectly and quickly. The shifty weather was as unreliable as always, and shipping labor and supplies back and forth cost a fortune.

This year would be even harder, to boot. They'd travel on snowmachines every morning from the Retreat to their dock by the ocean. There, they'd restore a lodge and an activity center after a storm had damaged both the exteriors and interiors.

Nobody wanted to do construction work in the dead of winter in Alaska. For several reasons. But they had no choice.

"Will you forget me?" Lani asked tearfully.

Kyle nearly rolled his eyes. "Laying it on a bit thick, aren't you?"

She shrugged dejectedly. "I'm used to losing people in my life…"

For the love of God.

Sniffle, sniffle.

"Lani," Kyle groaned in frustration.

Sniffle, sniffle. Those Bambi eyes…

"Fine!" he snapped and stood up. "Pack your damn bags!"

It was crazy how fast Lani went from saddest little thing to jumping on her bed. "Woot! I love you, Uncle Kyle!"

Kyle's dad thought it was hilarious and called him out on being whipped.

*

Logan had been worried about this trip for weeks for Justin's sake.

He should've known better. Once they'd landed in Anchorage, Justin's eyes had grown large at the sight of the snowy mountains. Then they'd continued up to Nome where Justin had *touched* snow for the first time. And the kid was over the moon. He rolled around in it, squealed in delight when Quinn helped him build a snowman, and screamed in protest when they had to go inside and check in to the motel.

They met up after and went out to get some lunch, and Justin was plastered to his favorite uncles. Quinn, particularly, who was working the perfect angle to make Logan move up here permanently.

Justin was on board. Logan wasn't.

"You wanna sit with me and Uncle Declan, buddy?" Quinn asked Justin as they walked into a diner.

"Yes, please." Justin took in each sight the way only a four-year-old could—with wonder and amazement and a completely open mind.

To Logan, it was just freezing. "I'm starting to regret Skyping with you guys so often," he muttered, sitting down at a round table between Quinn and Declan. "Justin likes you too much."

"Pretty sure that's Quinn's agenda," Declan chuckled. As if he wasn't bad himself. Facing Justin, Declan told him about all the cool stuff they could do at the Retreat—from dog sledding and ice fishing to swimming in the pool and making their own snow cones with the cleanest snow in the whole world.

"Wow," Justin whispered as Quinn helped him with his jacket and hat.

Logan smiled in spite of himself. Seeing his son enjoying himself meant a shit ton, and Logan had to admit it was nice with a change of scenery. The past two years had been filled with so much work and so many adjustments that when Quinn had called and, without fucking around, said they really needed extra help this year, Logan hadn't hesitated.

Pam and Hank were a godsend, but it didn't feel awesome for a thirty-one-year-old man to live with his pseudo parents.

"I have to take this," Declan said, bringing out his buzzing phone. "Order for me." He kissed Quinn before heading out.

A waitress walked over shortly after that, so they placed their orders, and Logan tried not to balk at the Alaskan prices.

"I know, dude. I know." Quinn could apparently read his mind. "Don't get me started on groceries. Makes me miss Publix."

Logan laughed under his breath and looked around them. "I don't get how locals can afford living here."

"We make more money." Quinn smirked.

We, he'd said. Logan shook his head, smiling. "You're one of the locals now, huh?"

Quinn shrugged. "It's home."

Logan wanted to feel that connected to a place someday, too. Unable to help himself, he tried to picture a life here. The week he'd spent at the Retreat a year and a half ago had been hysterical; they'd had a great time together in the wilderness, but Logan wasn't sure he could pull off living like that.

Okay, enough. Logan pushed away those thoughts and changed the topic. "So who's coming this year? I'm guessing John and Alex."

Quinn nodded. "They're already at the Retreat with Kiery. Patrick's staying, too. The storm really destroyed the dock. Oh, and Kyle. He's flying down from Barrow today." He checked his watch. "Actually, he's probably landed now."

Logan nodded and looked down, irritated with the images that popped up in his mind. He'd confessed to Quinn almost two years ago that he was *confused* about certain things, except it hadn't been too difficult to ignore. That was, until he met Kyle Shaw that May in Anchorage. Logan felt unnerved by the guy, and the week up at the Retreat had only made it worse. Whether Kyle was covered from head to toe or showing off his toned body full of ink in the indoor swimming pool, Logan got flustered and aroused.

It hadn't helped when he'd learned from Quinn that Kyle was bisexual. If anything, it had made it more difficult for Logan to keep his shower fantasies about women.

He clearly needed to get laid. It had been ages. Living with Hank and Pam, working, taking care of Justin…he didn't have a whole lot of time left for a social life. And now he was gonna spend three months with a bunch of dudes? Christ.

"Here we go, guys." The waitress returned with their food. "If there's anything else, just holler."

Logan put his salmon sandwich away for now and offered to help Justin cut up his hamburger.

"No, it's okay. I've got this," Quinn assured him. "Justin and I are gonna be best friends this winter. Ain't that right, buddy?"

"Yeah," Justin laughed and munched on a fry.

Logan tried to relax. What Quinn had said was true. He'd turned out to be a decent handyman—which Logan was only a little surprised about—but a lot of the work this year required more than that. So Quinn would take on lighter tasks while watching Justin.

"Eat. Unclench," Quinn told Logan pointedly. Then he looked at something behind Logan, and it turned out to be Declan. "You don't look happy."

"No." Declan sat down and sighed heavily. "One of our orders won't go through in Anchorage, and I can't fly down to check it out. I have three more shipments to approve here, and Pat can't leave the Retreat."

"What kind of shipment is it?" Logan asked.

Declan picked up his burger, though he didn't appear very hungry. "Heaters and timber."

"I can do it," Logan offered with a shrug. Quinn was one of the few people he was comfortable enough leaving Justin with, and it sounded like a quick trip. He could fly there now and then be on the first flight back tomorrow morning. "Unless you wanna send Valium boy over there." He jerked his chin at Quinn.

"My middle finger. Picture it," Quinn said flatly. "And when're people gonna learn it's only the bush planes I don't like? Y'all don't see me bitching when we go from here to Anchorage. So excuse me if I indulge in the barest amount of magical medication when we fly with Mitch."

"Easy, baby," Declan chuckled. "You're in luck. Mitch's son is flying us up later, and his plane is bigger. Otherwise, we wouldn't fit the cargo." Next, he slid his gaze to Logan. "I'd really appreciate if you could go with Kyle."

Hold the fuck up. "Kyle?" It suddenly felt like Logan had a noose around his neck.

Declan nodded. "I texted him. The heaters are kinda his area, so he's gonna check those—make sure it'll be warm enough in the lodge to work full time, but not so warm the heaters expand the timber or take up too much fuel." Yeah, one of the reasons construction was a bad fucking idea in the winter. The materials shrank and expanded with the weather. "He's not as experienced with the timber, though. And it's a temperature issue there, too. Our guy in Anchorage isn't sure the wood is cold enough because it just arrived from the Lower 48. So if there's any risk of expansion, we gotta let the timber be outside for a few days before we can get started. Time we don't have."

"All right." Logan got it. They weren't problems a construction worker ran into in Florida, but he got it. "Want me to measure it?"

Quinn burst out in laughter, to which Logan and Declan looked at him strangely.

"Oh, come on!" Quinn laughed. "Warm wood, cold wood, growing wood, *measuring* wood?"

Declan groaned and pinched the bridge of his nose, though he was grinning, too.

Logan chuckled. "What are you, fourteen?"

"*Yes.*" Quinn smirked, glee in his eyes.

Shaking his head, Logan took a bite of his sandwich. Declan leaned over Justin to whisper something in Quinn's ear, and judging by the flush on his cheeks, Logan didn't wanna know. But it did remind him of how badly he needed to get laid, and maybe he could go to a bar tonight in Anchorage to deal with that issue.

CHAPTER 2

"Thanks. If it could make it on the next plane back to Barrow, that would be great." Kyle signed the release form and then brought out his phone to text his dad.

As soon as they had landed in Nome, Kyle had run into an old friend—a pilot. And what with the insanely strict alcohol laws in Barrow, there was nothing like making a little extra money on some good old-fashioned bootlegging. It just had to be done with a pilot who didn't care about the cargo.

"No problems. Will your old man pick it up?" Erik asked. "Been a while since I saw him."

"He'll probably send our neighbor—Roger," Kyle answered. "Dad broke his hip on a fishing trip."

"That sucks, man." Erik winced. "Well, you take care. I think your niece is itching to get out of here."

Kyle peered behind him and saw Lani and Wolf sitting on the concrete floor between two bush planes, and they were looking toward the exit of the garage bay.

"It's been at least a year since she saw the outside of Barrow," Kyle chuckled. For the first time, he was genuinely glad he'd let her tag along. Last time she went with him anywhere, it was to his place in Pinnuaq Bay. "Okay, I'll see you around, Erik."

"Take care, bud."

Kyle walked over to Lani and Wolf and picked up their luggage—one big backpack, two duffels, and one crate. "We ready?"

"I was born ready," Lani said cheekily. "Should I put Wolf's leash on?"

"Nah." Kyle had trained his pup better than that. Wolf obeyed every command, regardless of how many people were around to distract him. "Let's check in at the motel, and then we can meet up with Declan and Quinn and get some chow."

Compared to Barrow, Nome was not only brighter, but also warmer. It was midday, which gave them a few hours of daylight, and both Shaws were dressed like it was spring. Thermals, camo pants, boots, and hoodies. Five, ten degrees was nice.

They got to the motel and checked in without issues, and on the way out again, Kyle texted Declan, finding out which diner they were at. They'd already messaged each other a little—about a trip to sign off on a shipment in Anchorage.

The entire walk over to the diner, Lani was like a pig in shit. She looked incredibly happy.

"I'm glad you're here, *miki*." Kyle winked at her when she looked up with a bright smile.

"Me, too."

Kicking some snow off his boots, Kyle opened the door to the diner so Lani could head inside. Then he pulled out Wolf's leash from one of the side pockets in his pants and tied the dog to a lamppost. There were already two other dogs near the entrance.

"I'll bring you back a treat." He patted Wolf's head before entering the establishment. He spotted Declan and Quinn and...huh. He recognized Quinn's friend from Florida, but the little child was new.

Kyle ran his fingers through his hair, knowing a cut was long overdue. If hair got in his eyes when he was out hunting, it was too long. "Come on, over there." He ushered Lani toward Declan's table, and they saw him when they were a dozen feet away.

"Look who it is!" Quinn was...carefree and happy.

Kyle grinned faintly and quirked a brow at Declan. "He on

Valium already?"

"For the love of…" Quinn grumbled.

"No, he made his coffee Irish," Declan said with a smirk. "Good to see you, Kyle. This is your niece, I assume?"

"Yeah…" Kyle placed a hand on her head. "Lani here sorta held me at gunpoint." That made Lani giggle and the rest chuckle. "Anyway, I know we're off to Anchorage, but she won't get in the way and I'll buy an extra ticket for her."

Declan waved that off. "Don't worry about it. You remember Logan, right? You'll be going with him instead." He went on to explain the situation and why Declan couldn't tag along, and Kyle nodded and shook Logan's hand.

Not much had changed with Logan Ward. He was still hot as fuck, all hard edges and warm colors. Kyle couldn't decide if he liked the trimmed beard or the brown eyes more, not that it mattered.

When they'd first met, they'd all gone out to a pub after dinner at Declan and Quinn's place, and Kyle and Logan had ended up going to the men's room at the same time. There, Kyle had casually asked if Logan was looking forward to the vacation up at the Retreat, and Logan's response had been to grunt something unintelligible and stumble into a stall.

During their vacation, whenever Kyle said anything, Logan had only offered clipped answers and hasty getaways.

Whatever Logan had against him wasn't Kyle's problem.

"Declan and I are leaving as soon as the shipments have been cleared," Quinn said. "We're bringing Justin with us, and Lani is welcome to join us, too. And Wolf—you've brought him, right?"

"He's outside," Kyle answered with a nod. He looked down at Lani. "It's up to you, *miki*. Either you come with me to the city or you go to the Retreat."

"Can I go fishing?" Lani asked hopefully.

"No," Kyle replied with a quiet laugh. "None of that until I get there."

She pursed her lips, thinking it over.

"I think we're just gonna settle in and maybe spend some time with the dogs." Quinn smiled at her. "There are new puppies if that matters."

"Oh, that matters," Lani said. "I'd definitely like to join you, please. Thank you for offering."

She could be polite to others, eh?

"She's a cutie." Quinn grinned at Kyle.

"You say that because you're not her uncle," Kyle replied dryly.

"Okay, so it's settled." Declan pulled out a set of keys. "You can stay at our apartment, of course. I'll head over to the airport with you. Hopefully, our food is there now, and I gotta get you tickets, too."

"You sure about this?" Logan asked Quinn, appearing nervous.

Could be one of two reasons, Kyle reckoned. One, he was uncomfortable leaving his kid. Two, he didn't wanna travel with Kyle.

Kyle had no fucks to give, so he went to the register to order some food to go. Lani was social and fearless, which was a relief. It allowed Kyle to be free of worries; plus, Lani was incredibly independent for her age. The elders on her mother's side of the family had taught her their traditions from an early age, and Kyle and his dad had always encouraged her to learn, grow, and adapt.

At seven, she was making her own seal oil and gutting the fish she caught. At eight, she exchanged her Barbies for a sewing kit and her own knife. At nine, she got her first rifle to practice with. At ten, she threw a fit if she wasn't allowed to go hunting with her family.

She did have an odd fixation with nail polish and princess games on her cell phone, but those were pretty much the only girly things she loved.

As the waitress got busy with their order, Kyle turned around and watched Lani talk animatedly with Quinn and Justin. Yeah, she would fit in just fine. That said, a few words wouldn't hurt, so Kyle whistled and got her attention. He jerked his chin, and she came running over.

"You gonna be good for Quinn and Declan?"

She saluted him. "Yes, sir." Then she grinned, excited. "We're gonna have a movie night in their cabin, and Quinn said he'd bring in the new puppies for the night—even though they just moved out to…the yard, or whatever he said."

"I'm sure you'll have a lot of fun." Kyle brushed a strand of hair away from her forehead. "If you need me, you can always call, okay?" She nodded. "Good. Don't go anywhere without asking permission and bringing Wolf. Oh, and dress like you would at home. Only Declan knows this is nice weather for us. Quinn would probably freak if he saw you in this up there." He tugged at her hoodie. "One last thing: keep in mind that Justin isn't more than three or four years old. Ask Declan where you can lock away your knife as soon as you get there. I'll make sure he reminds you, too."

"I won't forget, *anatchiaq*." She mussed up her hair again.

"*Akkaaka*," he corrected her. "*Anatchiaq* is for maternal uncle."

"Okay." She smiled. "Was there anything else?"

"Yes." He dipped down a bit and gave her his cheek.

Lani took the hint, giggled, and kissed his cheek. "*Nakuaġikpin*," she sang.

Kyle chuckled. "I love you, too. Anything you want me to bring with me from the city?"

She hummed and tapped her chin. "Marshmallows?"

He was pretty sure they already had those at the Retreat, but he made a mental note to buy a bag for her. "Got it."

*

Logan slid into his window seat, admittedly still a little shocked by all the hunting gear Kyle had handed over to Declan before they boarded. Two rifles, two handguns, ammo, a whole case with knives, fishing gear, an ax, a big container with frozen fish eggs—*seriously, what the fuck?*—chains, rope, wires, duct tape for some reason, and small traps. And even with that going off to the Retreat, Kyle had checked one knife, one rifle, a pair of binoculars, and an additional handgun to bring with him.

Declan hadn't even blinked, so Logan wondered if it was normal.

He had nothing against hunting, as long as children weren't exposed to it, and he was curious about it. Having gone with Quinn and one of his uncles to the practice range a fair bit at home in Florida when they were younger, Logan had to admit the prospect of learning how to hunt appealed to him.

He wanted to ask Kyle about it, though something held him back every time he tried. The man intimidated Logan, and he didn't even know why. Kyle had a couple inches on Logan's six feet, but they had the same toned build. Maybe it was Kyle's expression. It seemed the guy was always on high alert. He came off as casual and relaxed, except there was something calculating about his eyes. Like he was always observing and waiting to strike.

You're being fucking ridiculous, Ward.

"Great," Kyle muttered from next to him. "Got a text from Declan. Patrick called from the Retreat, and there's a warning for complete whiteout tomorrow. Declan's gonna try to get us out of Anchorage earlier; otherwise, we'll get stuck."

"What's earlier than the earliest flight?" Logan asked. It was stupid; he was more thankful for the icebreaking between him and Kyle than worried about some blizzard.

"One that's there just for us," Kyle replied, leaning back and closing his eyes. "Wake me up when we get there."

So much for continuing the conversation.

Why did Logan even care?

*

It was late when Kyle unlocked the door to Declan and Quinn's place, and he wanted nothing more than to go to bed.

The trip hadn't been wasted, though. The heaters had been mixed up with another model, so Kyle had adjusted the order while Logan had been on the phone with Declan to compare the digits on the timber.

Everything had been taken care of now, including a quick trip to Costco.

Kyle wasn't gonna turn down the opportunity to buy a gallon of milk that didn't set him back ten bucks. Really, it was cute how

Alaskans below the Arctic Circle complained about costs.

"You can take the guest room. I'll be on the couch," Kyle told him.

"I'm not going to bed yet," Logan said. "So if you wanna crash now, you can take it. I'm headin' out."

That made Kyle pause in the middle of the living room. "Errands for Declan?"

Logan shook his head no as he stripped off his snow pants, leaving him in jeans. "I haven't had a day off—unless my son's been around—since I was up here last time. I need to find a bar."

Kyle got the message. Loud and clear. He snickered and sat down on the couch, stretching lazily. "Bring her back here and we can share her." It was a joke. For the first time in his life, *really* a joke.

He'd never been a saint. In fact, up until two years ago, he'd been somewhat of a manwhore. He didn't have an endless list of hookups, but he'd definitely fucked around and then some. It had gotten old, though. After seeing what Declan and Quinn had, shit had changed. Kyle had calmed down. Maybe he'd also become a bit withdrawn.

"You look like you can't breathe," Kyle told Logan.

Or maybe like he was constipated.

"What?" Logan masked his obvious discomfort at Kyle's joke by throwing him an irritated glare. "I can breathe just fine."

Kyle shrugged. "I was only kidding about the sharing. You have fun." He grabbed the remote and turned on the TV.

Hopefully, a game could distract Kyle from the voice that urged him to go out, too. Old habits and his dick died hard, and seeing Logan all flustered was sorta hot.

15

CHAPTER 3

Four beers and four shots of Jack later, Logan was three sheets to the wind and feeling better. He was himself. Comfortable in his own skin, popular with the ladies, and there was no Alaskan motherfucker named Kyle around to cut his IQ in half.

Logan gritted his teeth, annoyed and frustrated. No one had ever rattled him that way, and it was fucking with his ego.

The blonde clinging to him would do. He was half-hard already, so fuck it. He wasn't gay. There was nothing to worry about.

"Wanna get out of here?" he asked the blonde. He recalled her name—it was...Alison or something. He kissed her neck and shifted his hand higher up her thigh, stroking it sensually.

"Yeah." Her voice was breathy and full of desire, reminding him that he usually knew what he was doing. He knew sex. He was good at it. "I just gotta check in with my roommates."

"Sure." Logan kept his mouth and hands on her while she called her friends, and he learned her name was Alyssa. Her perfume was a little strong—too sweet—but she was a knockout, no doubt. Big rack, legs that went on for days, sexy curves, nice ass.

"Your place or-or mine?" Her breath caught when Logan brushed over the fabric of her panties. Praise Jesus for short skirts.

"Bring her here and we can share her."

Fuck that. It was only a joke, like Kyle had said. And if it weren't, Logan definitely shouldn't bring the chick to Quinn's place. They should go to her apartment, even if there were roommates.

"Your call," he told her. "Wherever you feel most comfortable."

That earned him a blinding smile. "Your place."

Logan shouldn't feel excited about that pick.

He wondered how far this could go…

*

Kyle was in the bathroom, having just gotten ready for bed, when he heard the unmistakable sounds of two drunk people stumbling around in the apartment.

He frowned at himself in the mirror, wondering where the pang of disappointment came from. And why. Good for Logan, right? He'd obviously scored like he wanted.

All Kyle wanted was to catch some sleep. Exhaustion was written all over his body. He scratched his chest, the only part of his upper body—not counting his head—that wasn't covered in ink. Two full sleeves, his back, neck, and a little along his ribcage, plus one design across his collarbone; it was a bit of an addiction.

He rubbed a hand over his clean-shaven face, waiting for the sound of Logan and the chick locking themselves into the guest room. But it didn't come, and Kyle was growing impatient.

Seeing as he didn't drink alcohol himself, he had even less patience for drunk people.

Resigned to tell them in person to get out of his way, he flicked off the light and left the bathroom. Then he wandered into the living room and found them making out on the couch where he was gonna fucking sleep.

Tilting his head, he zeroed in on Logan's hand up the chick's skirt. The muscles in his arm flexed as he finger-fucked her, and judging by her moans, he was good at what he was doing.

Kyle's cock thickened under his sweats that hung low on his

17

narrow hips, 'cause he was still a red-blooded male. He was also bi, and having one of each getting it on in front of him would've made the old Kyle jump in and join the party the second they got here.

"Oh my God," the woman whimpered. "So, so, so close."

She started trembling, and Logan redoubled his efforts. He seemed to avoid her mouth and kissed her neck and exposed tits instead.

He was at least half-hard in his jeans, Kyle could tell. Or he had a less-than-impressive dick and was rock hard.

The woman pulled down her top a bit more and then unbuttoned Logan's shirt to reveal a perfectly toned chest with a sprinkling of chest hair. It matched his brown hair that was buzzed short on his head.

Kyle's mouth became dry at the sight of him.

Soon, the chick stiffened and cried out, her head falling back.

Kyle reckoned that was enough. He'd been a fucking gentleman, waiting until she got off, but now they could carry on in the guest room.

Then he stopped himself. Why even go there? No, screw it. He could take the guest room. The two on the couch were busy, so Kyle turned around and aimed for the bed in there.

Once the light was switched off, he lay down, and not five minutes had passed before he heard Logan and the girl come closer in the hall outside.

The woman giggled at something.

"*Shhh, we gotta be quiet,*" Logan chuckled.

Kyle rolled his eyes and sat up, scooting over to the edge of the bed. It was clear they were about to open the door, and they did.

Logan switched on the floor lamp near the door and blinked drunkenly at Kyle.

"I didn't know you were here, Kyle," he slurred.

Kyle narrowed his eyes. "Where did you think I was? On the couch?"

"Oh, hi…" The chick eye-fucked Kyle. "Are all guys from Florida so hot?"

Kyle didn't reply. For one, he wasn't from fucking Florida.

For two, he was busy studying Logan. Something was up. Kyle had told him earlier he'd take the couch, and then Logan had ended up there. Now they were here in the guest room, and there was no reason for Logan not to conclude the bed had been taken.

"I'm Alyssa." The girl—Alyssa—walked over and sat down next to Kyle on the bed. Her big blue eyes were still trained on his torso. "Are you a hunter?" Her fingers came closer and ghosted along several tats along his sides. A wolf, howling in the night. A man on stormy seas, harpoon held high. Lani's name and birthdate inked on the body of a polar bear cub. "Your daughter?"

"Niece." Kyle didn't look away from Logan, whose own stare was unreadable.

There was a hint of hesitation as Logan stepped farther into the room, but his actions were enough for Kyle to know where this was going. He had to admit he was shocked Logan would go there, and now he was intrigued.

Straight men tended to prefer threesomes with two girls, not two men. It wasn't some unwritten rule though, so Kyle didn't read into it. But that didn't mean he wasn't curious. Because Logan had been nothing but standoffish with Kyle.

"Fuck, you're both so incredibly sexy," Alyssa said, biting her lip.

Logan lifted a brow at Kyle—a silent question—and pulled out a few rubbers from his back pocket and tossed them on the bed.

Well. Kyle supposed he could take a break from his celibacy.

He shifted in Alyssa's direction and kissed her before there could be any lingering silences that turned shit awkward. He swallowed her gasp and moved his hand up to push down her top the way it had been in the living room. Her breasts spilled out, and in Kyle's periphery, he saw Logan stepping closer and unzipping his jeans.

She moaned and reached out to stroke Logan's cock, which definitely wasn't less-than-impressive. He was long and thick, and Kyle wished for a moment that Logan was into guys, too.

"God," Alyssa breathed out as Kyle pinched her nipples. "I want—I want you to fuck me, Logan." She got up on all fours on the bed, facing the edge, and her left hand reached over to feel Kyle's crotch. "Holy shit. I want this beast in my mouth."

Though he usually preferred to be the aggressor when it came to women, it wasn't really about her this time. He was honest with himself; he wanted to see how this played out with Logan. So instead of taking charge, Kyle leaned back against the mattress and let Alyssa pull down his sweats.

In the meantime, Logan grabbed a condom and climbed onto the bed, positioning himself behind Alyssa.

"Take a rubber, hon." Kyle sat up a bit so he could hand her one. He didn't wanna get sucked by a stranger without protection.

She pouted at him. "But I want to taste you."

He pointed to his hard cock. "Get to sucking instead."

It was clear she wasn't thrilled with his tone, though Logan did a thorough job of derailing her thoughts by ramming his cock inside her pussy.

Alyssa cried out and dug her fingernails into Kyle's thigh. Seconds later, she was suddenly eager to roll the condom onto his cock, and she looked desperate for it.

She sucked like a pro, too.

Kyle grunted and fell back again, the side of his face brushing up against Logan's thigh. Kyle had a perfect view of Alyssa's ass and how Logan's dick disappeared into her pussy, yet it was Logan's goddamn leg Kyle was drawn to.

Placing a hand on Alyssa's head, Kyle guided her over his cock while he stared hungrily at Logan fucking her.

As the minutes passed, Kyle kinda lost the concept of boundaries. If he was in bed with someone, it wasn't natural to avoid that person. So somewhere during the fantastic blow job, Kyle tilted his face and stifled a groan by sinking his teeth into Logan's thigh.

"*Fuck*," Logan growled. He sped up, and as Kyle broke through his haze, he felt Logan's fingers weaving through his hair. Holding Kyle in place. "Alyssa, I want you in the middle of the bed. Kyle, you should try her pussy."

Turned on and ready to explode, Kyle moved around on the bed as the others did the same. The two men ended up on either side of Alyssa, Kyle at her back and Logan to her front.

"I want it hard," Alyssa pleaded.

Kyle lifted her leg and shifted closer, then shoved his cock deep inside her. *Oh fuck, yes.* His eyes closed for a beat, the pleasure washing over him.

When he opened his eyes again, Logan was stroking himself off near where Kyle was pushing in and out of her, and the two were making out. Yet, Logan's eyes were fixed on Kyle.

Kyle clenched his jaw and slammed into Alyssa, causing her to gasp and break the kiss. It gave him the chance to take over. He kissed Alyssa hard, fueled by Logan's predatory stare.

Every time it was the other's turn to make out with Alyssa, Kyle and Logan inched closer to one another.

"Almost there," Alyssa whimpered.

Wanting to get her off faster, Kyle moved a hand down her front and circled her clit. The back of his hand touched Logan's cock, and if anything, Logan welcomed it. Logan cursed and rubbed the head of his dick along Alyssa's slit, and Kyle looked down as their erections slid together every time he pulled out.

"Jesus Christ." Logan was out of breath. "Kyle…"

Lifting his gaze, Kyle saw their faces were only a couple inches apart.

Alyssa dug her head back into the pillow and cursed as her orgasm claimed her.

Driven by pure desire, Kyle threw caution to the wind and closed the last distance. He pressed his lips to Logan's, half-expecting the guy to freeze up. Logan did the opposite. He groaned and cupped the back of Kyle's neck, quick to deepen the kiss.

Fuck, he hadn't prepared to be this affected by Logan. Kyle never lost control, but his head was swimming in lust now. His needs ruled him. Somewhere in the back of his mind, he registered that Alyssa had collapsed and was trying to catch her breath.

Like a flip of a switch, she stopped existing for Kyle. Maybe it was the same for Logan, because they gravitated toward each other with force. Meeting somewhere in the middle, they kissed each other aggressively until Logan tried to pull Kyle over to his side.

Kyle understood what Logan wanted and rolled over the

woman, ending up on top of Logan.

"God, yes." Logan palmed Kyle's ass roughly and pushed their cocks together. "I need—fuck, I'm not gonna be able to... I need more."

Kyle chuckled huskily and brushed his lips over Logan's neatly trimmed beard, hooked on the soft rasp of it. He had a feeling Logan wasn't very experienced with guys, so he decided to just roll with it. He'd definitely get them off.

"Hold on." He left a little space between them and wrapped Logan's hand around their cocks—well, as much as his fingers reached. Then Kyle began to move. *Damn, that feels good.* He returned to kissing Logan, who'd gotten the hint. "That's it." Kyle kissed him deeply, stroking their tongues together as they fucked Logan's fist.

"That is so hot, you guys... Anything I can do to help?"

Logan mumbled a curse and then sucked in a sharp breath when Kyle reached lower to massage the spot under Logan's tight sac.

"Can you trust me for a little while?" Kyle murmured, and Logan nodded quickly. "Keep your eyes on me." Logan gave another nod. Bringing his hand up again, Kyle slowly pushed two fingers into Logan's mouth before kissing him around the digits. Their tongues swirled around until Kyle deemed them soaked enough. Then he slipped his hand down to Logan's ass to gently circle his hole. "I won't go too far."

"I want it." Logan grunted and captured Kyle's mouth with his. He also tightened his grip on their cocks to stroke them harder. And when Kyle pushed his middle finger inside him, all Logan did was let out a low, drawn-out moan.

"I can suck you off, you know. Both of you—either of you. Logan? Kyle?"

"Fucking beautiful," Kyle groaned.

"*Fuck.*" Logan's eyes flashed open, and Kyle knew he'd found his prostate. "More—fuck me. I want you to fuck me."

Kyle wasn't so sure.

"Guys?"

"Don't make me beg." Logan smirked, though vulnerability

22

shone through in his eyes. "It's been a while, but…fuck. I need it."

Been a while? "You've been taken here before?" To emphasize, Kyle slammed three fingers into Logan's ass.

In the back of his mind, he registered the closing of a door and heels clicking away.

"Fuck!" Logan groaned. In pain or pleasure, Kyle couldn't tell. "Yeah," he panted. "Fuck me. There's a small packet of lube in my wallet."

All right. If the man had been fucked before and carried lube with him, Logan obviously wasn't as inexperienced as Kyle thought. And Kyle could stop playing nice guy and take what he wanted.

He crawled over the bed and reached down to get Logan's pants from the floor, tossing them to Logan. He retrieved the lube while Kyle replaced his condom with a new one.

Logan shuddered violently as Kyle got between his thick, muscular thighs.

"I'm ready." Logan stilled Kyle when he was about to slide his fingers inside Logan's ass again. "I'm ready."

And fucking eager.

Kyle clenched his jaw, suspicious but too fucking turned on to overanalyze. He coated his cock with lube and positioned himself. Keeping their gazes locked, Kyle slowly pushed inside.

Logan tensed up and sucked in a quick breath, his teeth gritted. "Oh my God…"

Jesus fuck. Kyle closed his eyes momentarily once he was buried balls deep. Logan was *tight.*

"Kyle—" Logan choked out.

Kyle opened his eyes, only to feel a tinge of panic when he saw Logan's wild gaze. He was fucking obviously in pain, and Kyle cursed and began to pull out.

"Fuck that!" Logan growled and held Kyle in place. "Don't stop."

"You drunk motherfucker." Kyle hung his head. So much for experience. "You haven't been fucked, have you?"

"Don't stop," Logan repeated pleadingly. "I gotta know."

Kyle hated Logan in that moment.

It wasn't fair to be put in this situation without choosing it. Kyle knew sex, and he knew Logan's first time shouldn't have been like this. Especially not when he was wasted.

"It's not as bad anymore." Logan went on, and he started stroking Kyle's arms sensually. "Please fuck me, Kyle." He kissed the top of Kyle's head, lingering and breathing in deeply. "You drive me fuckin' nuts. I can't act normal around you—I…I had to know."

Kyle didn't know exactly what Logan was rambling about, nor did Kyle wanna be used in an experiment on whether or not Logan was into men. 'Cause that was what it sounded like.

On the other hand… Kyle shifted inside Logan and groaned internally at the immense pleasure. Maybe he could at least turn Logan's first time into a good one.

Kyle lifted his head and looked Logan in the eye. "You've been a standoffish, awkward moron since we met, and now you want me to fuck you?"

"Meeting you—it threw me off guard." Logan's jaw ticked with tension beneath his beard. "I felt somethin', all right? I didn't know how to act, and it freaked me out—"

Kyle cut him off with a hard kiss. Logan's words mattered too little while he was drunk, so Kyle decided to just make this a good experience—for both of them.

Focusing solely on Logan, Kyle drew the lust back into the room. With passionate kisses, slow thrusts, grinding bodies, and sensual strokes, tense muscles loosened, and Kyle got Logan to forget about the subsiding pain.

"How do you feel?" Kyle murmured huskily. His breathing hitched as he pushed forward. With one hand, he rolled the condom off Logan's half-hard dick and stroked him firmly.

"Better—good." Logan swallowed and then moaned as Kyle angled himself for a deep kiss. "Oh, Christ."

It didn't take more than a couple minutes before Logan was rock hard and slick with pre-come in Kyle's hand.

"Your cock's fucking perfect." Kyle stared down at it, stroking it upward to see the shade of the flesh darkening. A drop of arousal beaded at the slit, and Kyle swiped the pad of his thumb over it. He let out a brief chuckle. "Jesus, it makes my damn mouth water." He slid his gaze back to Logan's flushed cheeks and brown eyes full of desire. "Have you thought about me sucking you off?"

He was curious—sue him. He wanted to know if it was true that he had made Logan react so strongly when they met. Had Logan fantasized about him? Jerked off to thoughts about the two of them?

Logan had starred in several fantasies for Kyle, though it wasn't until tonight he'd learned that Logan desired men. And Kyle didn't go after straight guys. Hell, lately he didn't go after anyone.

At first, it didn't look like Logan was gonna answer, but determination tightened his features. "More times than I could count."

God*damn*, that was hot.

"What about fucking me?" Kyle sped up a little, needing it. "Have you stroked yourself off thinking about pushing this cock in and out of my ass?"

Perspiration started to glisten on Logan's torso, and he nodded quickly. "Yeah."

Fuck, yes.

Kyle was losing it.

"And this?" He thrust forward harder now, his balls slapping mutedly against Logan's ass. "Have you finger-fucked yourself wondering what it would be like to have my cock inside you?"

Logan hissed and began meeting every push. "Yes." A groan escaped him and he dug his head back against the pillow, arching into Kyle. "Christ—*yesss*."

"How many fingers?" Kyle gathered Logan's hands above them on the pillow, pressing them down against the mattress and fucking his tight ass in earnest. "Two? Three?"

"Two," Logan gritted out. "Oh shit, I'm close—"

Kyle dipped down and stole a hungry, openmouthed kiss. Then he broke the connection and slid his nose along Logan's jaw, down to the warm crook of his neck.

"You should've gone with three or four," he whispered in Logan's ear. He stopped stroking Logan's cock, wanting to hear him beg. "Two is kind of adorable."

"You sadistic bastard, get me off." Logan whimpered—fucking *whimpered*—and it caused Kyle's orgasm to surge forward. "Come on, Shaw. Please—I need to come."

Kyle moaned when he felt Logan quivering beneath him. His ass clenched around Kyle's cock, and it was all he could take. Fisting Logan's erection again, Kyle stroked him off as hard as he fucked him.

"Let go." Kyle barely recognized his own voice. "*Fuck*—" He growled and rocked into Logan's ass, both their climaxes taking over. The warm stickiness of Logan's come coated his abs and Kyle's hand, and the smell of sex made Kyle's orgasm even more powerful. He filled the condom with his release, for the first time in his life wishing there was no latex between him and his sex partner.

It'd been years since he was with a man, and Logan Ward was probably the hottest of them all.

"So sexy," Logan mumbled, nipping at Kyle's neck. "This was...fuck." He let out a breathy laugh. "I can't believe I did this."

Me, either. Kyle stayed where he was for another moment, willing for it to last. Sooner or later, shit was gonna get awkward—he was sure of it.

"Don't get weird on me," Logan said quietly as Kyle rolled off him.

Kyle chuckled wryly under his breath and left the bed. "That's your job." He threw away the condom in a small wastebasket, pulling it out slightly from behind the nightstand so he wouldn't forget to take the bag with him tomorrow. "Tomorrow morning when you wake up—*sober*—you'll get weird."

"I don't think so." Logan smiled uncertainly and grabbed a box of tissues from next to the bed. After he cleaned himself up, he got under the covers and held them up for Kyle to get in, too. *All right, then.* "I still wanna—" He stopped abruptly and frowned at the space next to them. "When did Whatshername leave?"

Kyle smirked and got comfortable, resting a hand under his head. It didn't escape his notice that Logan was checking out his bicep and the ink there.

"Around the time you begged for my cock." He stretched

lazily.

He didn't believe everything was gonna be all hunky-dory when the sun rose, yet he hoped. He couldn't help but hope that Logan was different. Unbidden thoughts of having more with Logan made Kyle gnash his teeth together, but it seemed ridding that crazy notion was futile.

Logan shifted closer and lay his head close enough for Kyle to feel his breath on his shoulder. It was as if Logan was testing the waters, and Kyle didn't have a whole lot of resolve left to break, so he moved closer too and draped an arm over Logan's middle.

With that simple movement, Logan appeared to melt into Kyle. He kissed Kyle hesitantly before closing his eyes, looking oddly content now.

"Goodnight, Kyle."

"Night, Ward."

CHAPTER 4

Logan stood under the hot spray in the shower, trying fruitlessly not to freak out. His head pounded—he hoped the painkillers would kick in soon—and throwing up hadn't helped all that much with his nausea.

Kyle was right. This was nothing Logan could handle right now.

I had sex with a guy. I begged a man to fuck me.

His sore ass would remind him all day.

You liked it, though.

A part of Logan did, yeah. The majority of his brain cells were screaming in protest.

To hell with his *curiosities*.

The second he'd woken up—fucking spooning Kyle—Logan had panicked.

He couldn't help it. It was indescribably overwhelming, and everything was making his skin crawl at the moment.

It was probably just right this minute, but nevertheless, right here, right now, he hated every single aspect of his life—except for Justin. His son had quickly become the light of his life, but everything else...? Logan despised it all.

Living with Quinn's parents. Working temp gigs, going from construction site to construction site. The confusion about his sexuality. Complete lack of social life. Loneliness. Not having Quinn around anymore. Being on the same street as his own parents who barely acknowledged him because he was a failure in their eyes. Trying to be a good dad.

Adding last night to the mix—something he knew he had initiated—was the last straw.

What the fuck was he gonna do?

Turning off the water, he stepped out of the shower and wrapped a towel around his hips. He could hear Kyle moving around outside the bathroom, and Logan's watch on the sink told him he needed to hurry. They had a chartered plane waiting to take them to Nome, where they'd meet up with Mitch.

The shipment had made it on a cargo plane last night, and now it was Logan and Kyle and a pilot. Yeah, shit was about to get weird.

Logan glanced at himself in the mirror as he applied toothpaste to his toothbrush, and the only thing he saw was age. Was he really only thirty-one? He felt more like fifty-one. Old and fucking hungover.

Control. Logan craved at least a semblance of it. Something had to give. Something had to feel *familiar*.

His sexuality and the thoughts he'd had about men the past few years…he could control all that, right? He wasn't ready to deal with it, anyway. The attraction to Kyle terrified him. Logan *had* to push that away. Same went for work. He had a job for the next three months, and he had one waiting for him at home if he wanted it. That meant—despite how much he hated temporary gigs—at least he had an income. It was uncertain, but not at this point. He could worry in a few months.

Lastly, he could be a bit more open-minded about where he ended up. He should listen to Quinn's spiel for once. Because what it came down to was *home*. A place for him and Justin. Logan hadn't felt at home in Sarasota since before he left the first time—hell, since high school.

Logan blew out a breath, slightly calmer now. *Control.*

He left the bathroom and got dressed before he gathered his things. There was no trace left of Kyle in the bedroom; he'd even made the bed, so Logan aimed for the living room and found Kyle in the adjacent kitchen.

Logan swallowed and clenched his jaw, staring at Kyle's muscular back. A wild river, fish, and a bear with its paw out to catch dinner were inked across his right shoulder blade.

Control. The eye-fucking had to stop.

"Coffee?" Kyle held up a thermos without turning.

Logan cleared his throat and dropped his bag in the opening to the hallway. "Sure, thanks." He walked over.

"I'm gonna shower real quick, and then we can go." Kyle tilted his head at Logan, his calculating gaze looking for...*something.* "How you feeling today?"

"Hungover," Logan said lamely. "Sore."

Kyle's eyes flashed with both amusement and concern at that.

Logan knew this was the time to apologize for last night and play it off as a drunken mistake. "Look. About last night..." He averted his gaze and picked up the thermos, occupying himself with pouring a mug.

Kyle shook his head grimly. "Guess I was right."

Logan cleared his throat. "I'm sorry—"

"Don't wanna hear it." Kyle's voice had grown cold. "We leave in ten."

He left, and Logan was pretty sure he'd never felt like a bigger piece of shit. Hollow, too. Fuck, he needed his son. Logan's eyes burned as he kept staring down the mug of coffee he couldn't imagine drinking. Unless he wanted to throw up again.

*

Kyle sincerely doubted Logan would strike up a conversation along the journey north, but in case the guy wanted to, Kyle made sure that option had flown out the fucking window. His expression was closed—all business. There was no way Logan would get the satisfaction of knowing he'd cracked Kyle's internal armor, if only for one night.

Didn't matter. The guard had been slammed right back up, and Kyle had no plans on lowering it again. Especially not for that motherfucker.

As they landed in Nome, Kyle took the lead, pretending Logan wasn't even there. He met up with Mitch, who asked if there was anything else the O'Connor twins would need at the Retreat.

"I checked with both Declan and Patrick," Kyle replied. "We're all set there."

"All right, then." Mitch clapped his hands together. "Let's get going. I'm sure you're itching to go hunting, kid."

Kyle smirked faintly and picked up his backpack, hoisting it over one shoulder. "Unlike my friends, I'm not used to store-bought shit." With his free hand, he grabbed his rifle case and the bag of stuff he'd bought in the city. "You southerners have it easy. But I got a good deal on milk and spices, so that's something."

Mitch barked out a laugh, and they walked toward his plane in the hangar. "Only a guy from Barrow would call us southerners."

"If the flip-flop fits," Kyle chuckled.

"Hey, now." Mitch grinned and wagged his finger at him. Opening the door on the passenger's side, he gestured for Logan to go in first so he could sit in the back. "How's little Ilannaq, by the way?" Mitch grunted as he handed Kyle's backpack to Logan.

"Growing up," Kyle responded. "She thought I was gonna let her skip school while we're here. I burst that bubble and introduced her to correspondence school."

Mitch laughed and adjusted the seat for Kyle. Then he jumped down again, and Kyle got in while Mitch went to open the bay.

It was gonna be nice to get back to the Retreat. Even with the man sitting behind him, Kyle was gonna make the best of his stay. He had good friends there, lots of work and wildlife to keep him busy, and he'd enjoy showing Lani the grounds.

Mitch returned and closed the door behind himself. "Any plans for the spring?" He handed Kyle and Logan headphones before he began taxiing out of the bay.

"Depends," Kyle said, adjusting the headphones. "I might head to the Interior late April. Villages around the Yukon usually need help for when the ice breaks. There's always some people who aren't prepared."

"Amen to that." Mitch grunted. "My boy's looking for more work, so if you run across someone who needs a pilot..."

"Of course." Kyle nodded.

The sun was breaking through the clouds as they lifted, reminding Kyle of the whiteout warning. He asked Mitch about the latest forecast and found out they were still expecting a big storm, but it was gonna hit later. Early evening.

Having volunteered as a search and rescue worker frequently in the past, that part of Kyle never left. With a whiteout warning issued, he wanted to get down on the ground and make himself useful.

*

"Okay, buckle up, boys." Mitch began bringing the plane down. "We got a bit of a crosswind, so it'll be a rocky landing. Be glad Quinn ain't here."

Kyle brought out his binoculars to check the horizon. It was clear at the moment, though there was definitely a storm brewing. It might even hit earlier.

"Who's that down there?" Logan asked from behind him.

Kyle directed his binoculars and looked down at the runway they were approaching, and he recognized Quinn's blue parka. There was a small figure, too. Justin. He looked like a garden gnome in his green snowsuit and pointy winter hat with flaps to cover his ears.

"Quinn and your kid," he muttered. He saw Quinn pointing toward the plane, and the child jumped and clapped his hands. Kyle's mouth tugged up a bit, and then he refocused on the perimeters.

He hoped Justin would grow up to be less of a douchebag than his dad.

"How good is Quinn with his gun?" Kyle zoomed in to see better. The Retreat's little forest was surrounded by a shrubby, snow-blanketed landscape, and Kyle could see nine or ten creatures edging closer to the forest. It wasn't caribou, and foxes didn't move in packs. Had to be wolves.

"Decent," Logan replied. "Why?"

"Decent's not gonna cut it." Kyle stowed away his binoculars and reached for the case that held his old M39 rifle. "Mitch, I need you to bring her down for me."

Mitch knew the area and its dangers, and when someone told him to land, he fucking landed. There was a valid reason, and he didn't question it.

Logan wasn't created from the same stock. "Dude, what's wrong?"

"Pack of wolves moving closer." Kyle attached the mag and then got out his short-range .22. Just in case. As the plane touched ground, he swiped up his binoculars again and hoped the pack was only lingering in the background. Unlike what Hollywood made the world believe, wolf attacks on humans were extremely rare. Except, these shits kept advancing, and they were doing it fast.

Not normal.

"Stop the fucking plane!" Logan snapped at Mitch. "That's my son out there!"

The plane bounced and skidded along the strip, and then Kyle saw both Kiery and Wolf running out of the forest, and it wasn't long before Declan appeared, too. He must've sensed something was up because of how their dogs reacted, and now he was trying to get Quinn's attention.

"Come on, come on." Kyle spoke under his breath. Quinn looked back; he must've heard Declan, and only a second later, Quinn brought out his pistol and aimed it toward the approaching wolves.

"They're running in fast," Mitch said grimly.

They were both thinking the same thing, Kyle was sure.

Rabies.

At fucking last, the plane lost enough speed for Kyle to jump out.

"Back off, Quinn!" Declan yelled, ready with his own rifle. "Kiery, halt!"

Kyle let out a sharp whistle as he ran closer, and Wolf positioned himself in front of Quinn and Justin, baring his teeth and growling furiously.

The wolves were some twenty yards away when Kyle threw himself onto the ground to be able to hold his rifle steady. He peered through the scope and took down the male leading the pack, quickly followed by the second. Declan shot another one as the remaining wolves scattered.

"Fuck," Kyle swore. He got off the ground and stalked toward the three dying wolves, and Declan did the same. Behind him, he could hear Logan cursing Alaska and fussing over Justin, which only made Kyle wanna punch him. Alaska wasn't like any other state. Humans and wildlife lived together—end of fucking story.

"This one's probably infected," Declan sighed. A kill shot to the neck silenced the wolf permanently.

"Yeah." Kyle eyed the animal. Foaming at the mouth was actually uncommon, and this one had it. Slackened jaw, too. Then he walked over to another wolf, and that one looked the same. "Not this one, though." The third didn't have any outward signs of rabies, though it meant little. Either he'd simply followed his alpha, or he'd been infected later.

"I'll have Pat bag them and tag them and send them off to Fairbanks." Declan pulled out his com device to radio his brother. "Were any shot in the head?"

Kyle shook his head no. If a rabid animal was shot in the head, their brains couldn't be examined at the lab in Fairbanks. Not that Kyle gave a shit. His mind was going in another direction.

"We have the rest of the pack to worry about now," he told Declan. "I'll head out in an hour. Tell the others to stay indoors."

"The blizzard, Kyle," Declan reminded him.

Kyle just shrugged and started trekking back to the plane where his stuff was. "I've been through worse!" He threw a smirk over his shoulder.

Quinn looked a little shocked, but Kyle had to admit he was adjusting to life in Alaska well.

Logan, on the other hand... He was furious.

"You sure you're okay, baby?" He studied Justin frantically.

"I'm fine," Justin mumbled, scrunching his nose. "Why do

you look mad, Daddy?"

Good question, Kyle thought. This was life up here.

Everyone should respect the power of the nature here and know the dangers that lurked, but blaming an accident on animals that had been here far longer than humans was goddamn ignorant.

"Motherfucker," Kyle muttered to himself.

He refused to admit his hostility toward Logan was caused by this morning's rejection.

CHAPTER 5

Logan was ready to bail. He was also ready to kill every wolf he set eyes on.

How stupid was he, bringing his four-year-old son up here?

Once he'd dropped off his bags in the room he'd share with Justin in the staff house, he headed downstairs again. Quinn was in the kitchen with Justin, John, Alex, and a woman Quinn introduced as Sarah.

"You okay?" Quinn asked cautiously.

Logan nodded with a dip of his chin, despite that he was so far from okay, and sat down next to his friend at the kitchen table.

"We usually don't get that much action up here." Quinn tried to joke.

Had Logan been here on his own, he would've brushed this off of him a whole lot sooner, but it all came down to Justin. He was only a child, for fuck's sake. He couldn't defend himself, and Logan hadn't been prepared.

Christ, had it only been this morning he'd promised himself to keep an open mind to Quinn's praise about Alaska?

Justin moved over to Logan's lap as the front door opened, and he asked if they could go out and play in the snow now.

It relieved the tension a bit in the kitchen, and John and Alex grinned at the boy.

"It's not safe outside yet," Logan murmured. "Maybe tomorrow."

Declan and Patrick came in from the cold, and if it weren't for Patrick having longer hair and less scruff, it would've been impossible to tell them apart.

"Where's Kyle?" Alex asked.

"Behind the house getting our traps," Declan replied. He grabbed a cup of coffee and leaned back against the kitchen counter. "Pat and I are gonna help out before the storm hits."

Quinn didn't like that idea, Logan could tell, yet no complaint was voiced.

"You need another hand?" John offered.

Patrick spoke up. "If you don't mind, could you help Sarah bring in the dogs? They should be safe behind their fence, but we don't want them even close to the wolves if they're rabid."

Logan had seen the dogs. The airstrip was connected to a path that went between the forest line and a row of cabins. After that, there were three large lodge buildings that framed a yard and snow-covered barbecue area. And attached to the back of the western building—close to Declan and Quinn's cabin—there was a fenced area and a shed full of Huskies in various colors and sizes.

"Let's do it," John said, glancing at Sarah, and they left.

Then Kyle came in from outside, followed by his niece walking down the stairs.

"Are you going out for the wolves?" she asked him.

"Yeah." Kyle nodded and stepped out of his boots to put on snow pants. "You wanna come with?"

What the fuck? Logan's eyes bugged out.

"Yes, please!" Lani was thrilled. "I'll go get ready!"

Logan and Quinn exchanged the same look of shock, but when Declan subtly shook his head, Quinn schooled his features. Seriously, was nobody gonna speak up? Had Quinn turned into some doormat?

"Are you fuckin' serious?" Logan blurted out, staring at Kyle. "You're gonna let a little girl go after rabid wolves with you?"

The silence that followed was heavy with tension, and everyone seemed to watch Logan and Kyle like a damn tennis match.

Kyle smiled, though it was cold and condescending. "Do yourself a favor, Ward. Don't talk about shit you know absolutely nothing about."

"She's a child," Logan argued impatiently. "You don't give a shit about putting her in danger?"

"Logan," Declan cautioned, "Kyle knows what he's doing."

Does Lani?

Kyle chuckled darkly. "If I wanted to put someone in danger, I would've asked *you* to come along." Then he looked up toward the stairs. Lani was joining him, and the two exchanged a few words too quietly for the rest to hear before they headed outside.

Logan was in disbelief.

Quinn cleared his throat. "I trust Kyle. I do. But Lani's only ten. Is it really safe?"

"She's probably better than John is, and he's good," Alex said. "Really, the only difference between Kyle's family and bush people who live alone in the woods is that the Shaws are part of a community. They're almost completely self-reliant—they live off the land."

"I get all that," Logan said, and he did. "But exposing children to dangerous animals and—shit, the rifle Kyle has looks like it belongs in Afghanistan."

Patrick's mouth quirked up. "I think the newer M39s are used by the marines or the navy, actually. And accuracy rifles are necessary here, too."

"Logan, Lani was born into this," Declan said patiently. "Kyle and Lani's elders take this very seriously. They live by traditions passed down for generations, and no one can survive here better than them."

Elders. As in Native people. Logan could obviously see Lani was part Native, and it still seemed incredibly reckless. Her heritage wouldn't make the dangers go away.

"That's incredible," Quinn said.

Logan shook his head at him.

Quinn noticed, and he chuckled. "Trust me, Logan. When I was new up here, I had plenty of freak-outs. Just ask the others. But it's a culture thing." He shrugged a little. "They live differently, and they start out earlier. I'm sure Lani's family would balk at some of the things we do in Florida—or city folk in general."

Declan was smiling at Quinn.

Logan hated to admit that Quinn's statement made sense. That said, he was still on edge. Kids with guns...there was something fundamentally wrong there. Having actually spent time in Iraq, Logan knew a thing or two about children and guns, and it would never look right.

He had nightmares sometimes about the year he'd lived in Iraq a few years ago. The buildings they restored and schools they built always ended up with new bullet holes.

Two years ago, Logan had been contracted for another year of construction in the Middle East, but he'd been forced to come home early when an ex had dropped a kid off at his parents' house. Logan had gone from carefree bachelor to single father of a toddler overnight, though at this point, he was only thankful. He loved Justin more than anything, and it had gotten Logan out of a war zone, too. Where children played with guns.

"You ready to head out, little brother?" Pat asked Declan quietly.

When Justin yawned, Logan saw his escape. He needed to think, and he wanted to be alone with his boy. So he said he'd be back in a while before he went upstairs.

He passed Kyle's room, which was open. Inside, Logan spotted hunting gear, winter boots with fur on them, sleeping bags, and survival kits. He shook his head, rattled and dazed, then continued into his own room.

"Time for your nap," Logan murmured.

"I'm not tired," Justin mumbled.

"Of course not." Logan cleared the bed and got under the covers with his son. "I am, though. Mind staying with Daddy for a bit?"

Justin let out another yawn and snuggled closer. "'Kay." His eyes drooped until they closed. "I like the snow."

Logan smiled and pressed a kiss to his forehead. "I know, baby."

As mentally tired as he was, Logan didn't find rest. Even after repeating Quinn's words to himself and agreeing that it was a matter of cultural differences and nothing else, he lay there and stared up at the ceiling, unable to relax.

It hit him that he hadn't thanked Kyle for being there today. The man had fearlessly jumped out of an airplane before it had stopped—just so he could *help*. He'd put himself between danger and the people Logan cared about most in the world, and Kyle had taken care of things. He and Declan.

I keep hitting new lows. Logan screwed his eyes shut and cringed at his own stupidity.

Knowing he wouldn't be able to sleep, he carefully left the bed and spent the next hour unpacking and getting everything organized. He was nothing close to OCD, but being more settled in helped against the sense of feeling lost.

Clothes in the closet, laptop set up on the small desk, towels and toiletries in the bathroom across the hall, a bag of LEGOs and Transformers under the bed, and Justin's two stuffed animals placed on the rocking chair by the window. Okay—three months. For three months, he had his own little home in this room with Justin.

It was something. Something that could hold him together.

Declan had offered to bring up a children's bed from the main house, though it wasn't necessary. The queen-sized bed in the corner was definitely big enough for both Logan and Justin.

"All right." Logan sighed to himself. Nothing left to do in here, and Justin was still napping. "Time to make myself useful."

He left the door open and walked downstairs. He hadn't been in hiding that long, yet a lot had changed in the kitchen. Only Quinn was there now, the table was set for dinner, soft rock music played on his iPod, and it smelled insanely good.

"When did you learn how to cook?" Logan asked, testing a smile. It sorta worked.

"I never sucked at it like you do," Quinn chuckled. He bobbed his head to the song and flipped salmon in a skillet. "You might wanna get out of those jeans. If they get wet, you'll be chilled to the bone in no time." Logan eyed the loose cargo pants Quinn was wearing. "Thermals and snow pants are the answer for outside, but I'm spending all day in here today, so..." He sent Logan a quick smile before focusing on the stove.

"Is it even safe to go outside?" Logan asked. He stepped closer and took it upon himself to cut up the asparagus. Chopping vegetables and throwing meat on a grill was the extent of Logan's knowledge in cooking. Unless grilled cheese sandwiches with charcoal flavor counted.

"Should be." Quinn nodded. "They're lookin' for the last two wolves now."

"They've already caught—" Logan's voice was cut off by a radio crackling on the other side of the stove.

"We have one, Kyle. Do you copy?" It was Patrick.

"So that's why you're calm." Logan cocked a brow at his friend. "You know they're safe because you're hackin' in to their frequency."

"It's not so much hacking as it's a press of a button on the right channel, but fuck yes." Quinn grinned. "If Declan's not all right, I won't be able to marry that bastard this summer."

Logan snickered and set the asparagus aside to do the carrots.

"Copy that." Kyle's voice mingled with the static of the radio. "I'm tracking the last one. Lani's on her way back, and she's got a gift. At least act grateful—I know it's not the standard gift for you guys."

That made Logan and Quinn look up.

Declan was next to speak up. "Of course. We'll be at the house in five."

Only, Lani arrived in less than two.

The door opened, and Logan heard two boots being kicked off before the little girl ran into the kitchen with a beaming smile.

And two dead birds. Big, fat, white, dead birds.

"Hi! I brought you something." She dropped the two birds on the counter right next to where Logan was chopping carrots. "Aren't they real nice and fat?"

Logan didn't know how to react. He watched dumbly as Lani

removed her thick jacket and rubbed her reddened nose. Tangled hair was pushed back and snow pants were kicked off.

"This is…this sure is somethin'." Quinn found words, apparently. "What've you got here, sweetie?"

"Ptarmigans," Lani said frankly. "It's my first kill without help from Uncle Kyle, and the next step to becoming a provider is to give it away. Uncle Kyle and my elders say so. So…here you go." She smiled again, and a blush covered her cheeks.

She was fucking cute.

"I'll pluck and breast it for you," she added.

"This is incredibly kind of you." At long last, Logan found his voice, too. "I bet your uncle is very proud."

To be honest, Logan was just in awe. This young girl was learning how to provide for her family. She was doing things Logan couldn't fathom. Things he was struggling with, and he was an adult.

"I dunno. He said good job." Lani shrugged. "I'm gonna try to find two more tomorrow. Then it'll be enough for everybody, and we can have it for dinner."

"You are one amazing little hunter," Quinn told her. "You mind teachin' me and Logan a thing or two?"

That was actually smart. If Logan wanted to do well here, he might as well get with the program. He'd be better at keeping Justin safe, too.

"You want *me* to be your *teacher*?" Lani dropped her jaw. "Oh my gosh, *yes*. I can do that. I can give you homework, and-and-and I'll quiz you!"

Oh, boy. Logan looked at Quinn and smirked wryly. "Back to school for us, buddy."

"Be gentle with us, Lani." Quinn winked at her. "It's our first time."

Logan stifled a laugh.

"Nature isn't gentle," Lani said with a tsk. "What we want is the mess of success!"

CHAPTER 6

The only good thing about rabid animals was that they lost all sense of self-preservation. If the wolves smelled food, they came running, making it easy to trap them. Kyle drove back toward the Retreat with the wolves he'd taken down and shook his head at the waste.

As Kyle killed the engine to his sled, Declan met up with him behind the main house. It was windy as fuck, the snow hit them in every direction, and the visibility was poor. Unfortunately, responsibilities didn't take a break just because the weather sucked.

The two men had to yell to hear each other over the wind, and they worked quickly so they could go inside. While Kyle severed the heads, Declan double-bagged the bodies, and then they had to clear a stock fridge in the workshop for the heads. Nothing would get shipped out of here today, anyway.

"Where's Lani?" Kyle called. His face was getting too cold, but he couldn't pull up his face mask after dealing with infected animals. His thick gloves were already coated in caked, half-frozen blood.

"Staff house!" Declan grimaced against a harsh blast of wind and shoved the last carcass into a bag. "Wolf and Kiery are in my cabin!"

Kyle nodded, blinking away frost that was gathering on his eyelashes. He was definitely glad he'd sent Lani home earlier. Only the edge of the storm was here, and it was already brutal.

So much for Alaska below the Arctic Circle being milder this winter.

As soon as they were done, they got rid of their gloves, and they stripped off their jackets and snow pants right outside the staff house. With clothes in a protective bag, they walked in like two icicles and immediately told Lani and Quinn to stay back.

"We gotta shower first," Declan explained. "I'll steal some extra clothes from Pat on his floor."

"I left clothes for you in the bathroom," Lani told Kyle.

"Thanks, *miki*." Kyle shuddered and ripped off his hoodie. "Can you lead the way? I don't wanna touch anything."

"I'll help you to Patrick and Nina's loft," Quinn offered to Declan.

Quinn and Declan walked up first since they were headed to the third floor, and then Kyle followed after Lani.

*

Kyle exited the bathroom feeling a whole lot warmer and cleaner. Dressed in sweats and a T-shirt, he passed Logan's room to go downstairs, only to come to an abrupt stop when Justin tumbled out. His hair was messy from sleep, and he was rubbing his eyes so he almost walked into the doorframe.

"Easy there, kid." Kyle stared at the garden gnome.

Justin yawned and looked up. And up. And up. "I napped."

"Okay." Kyle's discomfort grew. He never knew how to act around tiny humans. Lani had always been different; besides, she'd had her parents up until she was five.

"Where's Daddy?"

Possibly getting it on with a guy so he can be an asshole tomorrow, too.

"I don't know." Kyle shrugged. "Maybe downstairs?"

Justin nodded, and then he fucking grabbed Kyle's hand. As if Kyle was gonna lead him down the stairs?

"This isn't really my thing." Kyle lifted his hand that Justin was holding on to.

"Okay. Come on." Justin began dragging Kyle toward the stairs. "Can we play in the snow?"

"No."

"Why?"

"Because there's a whiteout." Kyle rolled his eyes. "You'd get lost in the woods in two seconds."

"Why?"

For fuck's sake. "Because there's too much snow for you to see. Everything is white."

"My daddy would get me."

"Ha!" That shit was funny, and he was laughing when they reached the kitchen. He untangled himself from the little gnome and walked over to the table where John and Alex sat. "Where's this kid's keeper?"

"I'm here." Logan entered the kitchen, wiping his hands on a towel. "Come here, baby. Did you have a good nap?" Judging by his expression, he'd heard Kyle laughing about Logan coming to Justin's rescue in a whiteout and wasn't pleased.

Kyle smiled. "At least I didn't say you'd die trying, which is probably more accurate."

Logan shot him an exasperated look.

"Am I missing something?" Alex asked.

"No..." John looked between Logan and Kyle. "There's definitely some hostility going on here. Is this because of Lani going hunting?"

"Who the fuck knows with that guy," Kyle chuckled. "He says one thing and then does the opposite."

"Kyle," Logan gritted out.

At that point, both Quinn and Declan joined them.

They had obviously fucked in Patrick's shower.

"Dinner should be ready any minute," Quinn said, checking the food on the stove. "Oh, Kyle—did Lani tell you about the ptarmigans?"

"No. Did you tell Declan about the teeth marks on his neck?" Kyle asked casually.

Quinn blushed.

Declan smirked. "Are you jealous, Shaw?"

Not about the teeth marks. Well, maybe that, too. But damned if he was going to make himself vulnerable in this crowd again. Getting shot down by Quinn and Sarah two years ago hadn't even stung. Kyle had seen two extremely attractive people, and he'd gone for it. He did feel bad about continuing to flirt with Quinn after he'd made it clear he wasn't interested, except Kyle had made up for it. It was all good now, thankfully. But Logan? *Fuck*, it grated on Kyle's nerves that he was still bitter about last night. Or rather, this morning.

Wanting to change the topic, Kyle asked about the ptarmigans Quinn mentioned instead. Kyle was proud of his niece. Not only had she found them herself, she had taken them down efficiently— no muss, no fuss—without ruining the best parts with bullets.

"She knows what she's doing." Quinn placed a plate full of salmon in the oven—maybe to be reheated. "We thanked her, of course. Then she showed us how to pluck it and get the best meat out."

"We?" Kyle cocked his head, hoping it wasn't Logan Quinn was referring to.

"Logan and me."

Great.

Kyle wanted to keep himself and Lani as far away from Logan as possible. Perhaps distance would help Kyle get over this…whatever it was. Infatuation? No, they didn't know each other well enough for that.

"Okay, we're just waiting for the salmon." Quinn started carrying over rice, vegetables, and drinks to the table. "Declan, can you get Sarah and Patrick? And where's Lani?"

"I'll go get her," Kyle said.

*

Logan's plan had been to rush through dinner and then ask to speak to Kyle in private, but that didn't happen. Firstly, because *holy shit*, the food was better than any other home-cooked meal he'd ever eaten. Secondly, because this was the first meal where everyone was gathered, and Patrick and Declan had work schedules to go through with them. Thirdly, because Logan was eternally grateful for the company he found himself with.

He had barely given it a thought, which was fucking stupid. He noticed it during dinner. It was a great group of men—and woman—all fairly close, and they were quick to include Logan in everything. Patrick and Declan also made sure to always include the children, something that wasn't really their responsibility. They ran a business up here, not a day-care center. Yet, they got everyone involved.

Growing up, Logan hadn't exactly had that, so it was nothing he took for granted. His mom and dad had pushed him toward premed so he could become a doctor like many others in his family. When that didn't happen and he came home with average grades, they lost interest in their own son and "assumed" he didn't want to go with them on family holidays and so on. He was no longer a Ward to be proud of.

Pam and Hank Sawyer, Quinn's parents, had given Logan what his own folks didn't. A sense of belonging. Unconditional love.

"Don't tell your mom, but this was better than her pot roast," Logan told Quinn.

Quinn laughed. "I *want* to tell her. That's some praise, man. But wait until Kyle or Sarah cooks."

"What's that supposed to mean?" Declan looked insulted.

"Oh, I'm a little better than Kyle, aren't I?" Sarah batted her lashes at Kyle.

"You wish, hon." Kyle snorted a quiet chuckle and poured himself and Lani more milk. "Quinn's got the swimming, so don't take the cooking away from me."

Logan raised a brow at Quinn.

"Don't you friggin' dare," Quinn warned. "I'm the number one swimmer around here, and that's not gonna change."

"Hold on, now." Alex narrowed his eyes. "Is there a possible bet here?"

Declan looked like he'd just solved a big math problem. "Was that why you didn't wanna go in the pool the week we were all here? Because Logan might beat you? When I suggested going to the pool, you decided on the hike instead."

"You're full of it," Quinn said. "Now, if y'all will excuse me, I'm gonna do the dishes. Get out of my kitchen."

"Are you any good?" Alex asked Logan.

Logan shrugged all casual-like and ran a hand over his head. "Pshhh, I don't know, man. The guy who *taught* Quinn how to swim back in the day was pretty fucking good."

Quinn scowled.

Declan smirked. "Was that by any chance you, Logan?"

"Hmm, now that I think about it, I believe it might've been me." Logan draped an arm around Quinn's shoulders. "Ain't that right? I taught you everything I know."

"The things I wanna say right now…" Quinn slumped his shoulders.

"Guess we'll have to bet on it one of these days." John nodded firmly before standing up. "Now I reckon we have dogs to let out of their shed. What do you say, Sarah?"

"Yeah." Sarah stood up, too. "Thanks for dinner, Quinn."

"Bring your compasses," Kyle told them. "Zero visibility out there. If the storm's still raging tomorrow, I'll draw rope between the buildings so no one gets lost."

"Good thinking," Patrick agreed.

Justin wanted to help Quinn, so Logan waited until Kyle was leaving the kitchen and followed him up the stairs.

"Kyle," Logan called. Kyle glanced over his shoulder, pausing outside his room. There was no response whatsoever, so Logan continued. "Can we talk? In private."

He was nervous and on edge, but Logan had gotten them both into this mess, and Kyle deserved an explanation.

"Depends." Kyle leaned his shoulder against the door, his flat stare only making Logan more uncomfortable. "Will you go back on it like some fucking child tomorrow?"

Ouch. Logan had that—and more—coming. "No."

"All right. Lead the way."

Logan ignored Kyle's bored look and opened the door to his

and Justin's room. Lani had mentioned watching a movie after dinner, so if she ventured up here, Logan didn't want to get interrupted.

*

Kyle followed Logan into his room and stayed close to the doorway.

"So, what do you want?" He folded his arms over his chest.

Logan paced for a while, looking too handsome for his own good. Kyle had noticed the man's confidence with the chick they'd screwed, but did he know how sexy he was to guys? Logan's ass in those jeans…his exposed forearms in that Henley with pushed-up sleeves…his hot-as-fuck beard, hair buzzed short, and—

Kyle clenched his jaw, pissed. He'd always been able to control himself. Now shouldn't be any different.

"I don't have all day," Kyle said impatiently.

Logan hung his head. "I'm tryin' to figure out what to tell you without boring you half to death."

Kyle kept staring. He wasn't an unreasonable man; he took care of his own and helped out whenever he could, though not when he was getting jackshit in return.

He didn't wanna be part of a dude's games of am-I-gay-or-not, and he absolutely loathed being judged for how he and his family lived their lives.

"First of all…" Logan looked up, tired yet determined. "Thank you for bein' there today—when we landed. What you did…it was selfless. I don't even wanna imagine what could've happened to Justin or Quinn if you hadn't been there."

It was getting difficult to stay indifferent now. Kyle nodded with a dip of his chin, not entirely comfortable with the praise. "No worries."

Logan shook his head and stuck his hands into the pockets of his jeans. "That's just it, though. Lately, I'm all about worries, and it's driving me fucking insane." One hand came up, and he ran it back and forth over his head a couple times. "I wouldn't have been able to defend anyone against wildlife here, and I showed my

appreciation by insulting the way you raise your niece. I was
ignorant about it, Kyle. I'm sorry. I'm not gonna lie—the thought
of givin' a child a gun doesn't sit well with me. Nevertheless, I
don't know enough about your culture, and comparing it to my
time in Iraq isn't fair."

Damn. If Kyle had wanted an apology, he sure got it, didn't
he? He hadn't expected that much, though.

Logan's words loosened the tension in Kyle's shoulders,
allowing him to feel a little better. Less ticked off. Less willing to
remain aloof. And it was less likely he'd be able to stay away and
not ask questions. Logan had been in Iraq? He didn't strike Kyle as
a soldier. Maybe the posture, the way those in the military always
came off as stiff, but…

"I'm sorry about this morning, too," Logan said quietly. "It
got too much for me."

Kyle scratched his bicep, thinking about how Logan had
phrased himself. Sorry about this morning, not about last night.
There was a pretty big difference there.

"What part of all this would bore me?" Kyle asked with a tilt
of his head.

Logan squinted, as if wondering where Kyle's mind was at,
and then he got it. "Oh. Uh…" He let out a hollow chuckle. "I
opted against giving you excuses for how the past two years have
fucked me up."

Kyle stared as he processed that. He knew Logan's kid had
entered the picture a couple years ago, but that couldn't be it.
Anyone who took a look at Logan would see that his world
revolved around Justin.

"Try me," Kyle told him. "Let's see if I get bored." He wanted
to know, dammit. For emphasis, he walked over to the desk and sat
down in the chair. "Hit me with your worst, Ward."

"Are you serious?" A crease appeared in Logan's forehead.
When Kyle just nodded, Logan blew out a breath and sat down on
the edge of the bed. "All right…"

Kyle waited.

Logan sat forward and rested his elbows on his knees. "I
don't know, guess I'm just tired." He scrubbed a hand over his

short beard. "Too much changed in a short period of time, and I haven't been able to settle in."

Kyle didn't know the details, just that Logan and Quinn were best friends and had lived together down in Florida for years. Then a kid showed up and Quinn moved across the country.

"Were you and Quinn ever...?" Kyle let the words trail off. Logan had never been with a man before, but perhaps feelings had been involved.

"No." Logan smiled faintly and made a face. "I tried to kiss him once, which was fuckin' weird. It was right before he moved up here. I was mindfucked and afraid to lose him—or rather, the last piece of normalcy." For reasons Kyle had no desire to decipher, he was glad there was no unrequited love or anything. "When it comes to guys...I don't know, I've wondered for a few years, I suppose. And I picked the worst time to explore." He rolled his eyes, seemingly at himself. "Is it okay if I blame you?"

Kyle frowned, confused. "How could last night be my fault?"

Logan shrugged and averted his gaze. "You made it impossible to stay away."

At that, Kyle had to grin. His mood had already lightened, yet this took the prize. It was nice to know it wasn't only Kyle who struggled with the attraction.

"Anyway." Logan cleared his throat. "I couldn't cope this morning in Anchorage. Between trying to be everything for Justin, living with Quinn's folks, not feeling at home, hating my job, and now coming up here...it was too much."

Kyle bobbed his head slowly, thinking. Logan certainly hadn't bored him. Instead, Kyle found the excuses valid, and he felt sorry for the man. Everyone deserved to have that one place that felt like home. Kyle was lucky and had several. Barrow was one of them— the biggest one. He'd been born and raised there. But he'd lived all over the state, and the only places he didn't like spending much time in were the cities. Anchorage, Fairbanks, Juneau, K-town, Sitka...he didn't like going there. A few weekends here and there were cool. Perfect time to catch up with friends and eat cheap. He just never lingered.

"Is Quinn trying to get you to move here?" Kyle wondered.

He'd heard Quinn tell some wild tales about the nature during dinner, and Justin had been soaking it up. Meanwhile, Logan had shot Quinn everything from eye-rolls and wry smirks to middle fingers and snorts.

"Yeah, he's workin' full time on that," Logan drawled. Mirth tugged at his mouth, though. He couldn't be too bugged by it. "We'll see. At this point, I'm not sure I care where I end up. I just want a place to call my own, more than temporary jobs, and opportunities for Justin."

"Stability," Kyle concluded quietly.

"Exactly." Logan nodded and looked down, fidgeting with a small tear in his jeans. "So…are we good?" He glanced up.

"Yeah." Kyle had no reason to be a dick now. Shame. If Logan wasn't being a douche and Kyle couldn't find the will to keep his distance, it was gonna get difficult in other ways. "We're good." He clapped his thighs before standing up. If he stuck around, he might push for more. He had to *try* to give Logan a wide berth. "I'll let your obvious hatred for wolves slide." He winked.

Logan scoffed. "They wanted to eat my son and best friend. I think my hatred is justified."

"They were sick," Kyle pointed out. "But don't worry, Ward. I have three months to educate your Lower-48 ass."

CHAPTER 7

As their work began, so did unfamiliar routines, and Logan spent the next several weeks consumed by a new lifestyle. They were governed by the harsh weather conditions, though most days they were able to follow their schedule.

In the rare moments he was by himself in his room, he was browsing search engines online for answers about his sexuality. He wanted to understand so he could accept. And he wanted to know why he couldn't control his attraction toward Kyle.

It hadn't taken him more than two or three days to figure out it was a lost cause.

"There's only one reason you're here right now, Logan." Declan chuckled, focused on the fish he was gutting. Next to him, John was baking bread. "I'm gonna have to speak to my brother about that damn schedule."

Yeah…everyone had learned Logan was pretty useless in the kitchen. So the days he was on kitchen duty, everyone had plenty of ribbing reserved for him.

However… "Y'all are gonna love the meals tomorrow." Since they worked by the dock, a fifteen-minute snowmachine ride away from here, all meals had to be brought with them. So with Logan on kitchen duty tomorrow, he had to cook it all today. The only reason Declan was here now was because of the day. It was Sunday, which meant they hung around the Retreat.

"Oh?" Declan looked up. "Did you become a chef in the past five days?"

"No, but—"

"But *I'm* here!" Lani sang, revealing herself from the hallway.

Exactly. Logan grinned and rested a hand on the top of Lani's head. "That's right. I recruited a li'l helper." He grabbed the bag of food they'd picked out from the freezer in the main house.

"Well, that's a weight off my shoulders," John said with a wink at Lani.

Lani didn't take her "teaching" position lightly, and Logan had learned a lot from the ten-year-old. The first week, his pride had taken a hit or two. Then, once he started viewing her as a teacher who knew her own land as opposed to a child, they were quick to form a unique friendship. She taught him about the wildlife here, and he helped her with her homework and told her stories about states and countries he'd visited. She enjoyed those.

Her next step was to introduce him to hunting small game and fishing, though Logan had requested—for all their sakes—that she give him some advice on cooking first. Plus, he wasn't ready to see her using a gun.

Additionally, hunting was nothing they could hide from Kyle.

They weren't exactly *hiding*, but most of these "lessons" took place when Kyle was either working or hunting. And Logan had to be honest with himself now; he wanted to impress Kyle, which had been Logan's first clue that he couldn't shake the attraction he felt. He was hooked on the Alaskan bad boy; however, Logan felt inadequate—a feeling he hated.

Logan didn't really believe anything would happen between them again, except with his fantasies only growing stronger, denial was slowly but surely being replaced by hope and crazy dream scenarios.

"Okay, let's get cookin'!" Lani announced. "Is Justin gonna help?"

"Ha!" Logan laughed and began unpacking the meat packages

Lani had picked out. "I fear my kiddo's forgotten me."

It was true. While Logan worked, Justin was attached to Quinn, and whenever they had time off, Justin was glued to the dogs. Daddy got the mealtimes where Justin talked a mile a minute about everything he'd seen, done, and heard.

"So, what're we makin'?" Logan washed his hands and then turned to Lani by the table.

"Don't let him do too much, sweetheart," Declan advised.

"I love you too," Logan deadpanned.

Declan puckered his lips and returned to the stove.

"Halibut!" Lani beamed and held up a big fish. "Two of these big boys should be enough for lunch. Then we have moose for dinner. First, filleting. I've shown you this, so here you go." She retrieved a knife from her little case.

Logan approached with caution while Declan and John watched in amusement.

Fuckers.

*

Patrick was in the workshop behind the main house when Kyle arrived back from a hunt with Wolf.

"You're saving us thousands of dollars, Kyle. I wish we could hire you for the entire menu when guests get here." Patrick grinned as Kyle tossed a hare and two foxes on a workbench.

Kyle smirked to himself and started skinning the hare. "If only that was legal, eh?" As a licensed subsistence hunter, he was only allowed to provide for his family and make trades. Monetary profit off the meat was illegal for him.

Kyle followed the laws *most* of the time. But Patrick had the Retreat's books to worry about, and it would be difficult to explain hundreds of pounds of meat and fish that didn't come from an official supplier.

For these three months though, Kyle was merely bending the rules slightly. His family had grown to include coworkers.

"Have you seen Lani?" he asked, placing the fur to the side. "I'm supposed to help her with some history project for school."

Bringing out a knife, he severed the head.

"Oh, we all sorta quizzed her earlier," Patrick answered. To help out, he got busy with the first fox. "Logan helped her out as usual, and then there were a few of us who asked her questions from the textbook. She's a bright one."

That was almost too much to process. Kyle stopped working and faced Patrick. "What do you mean 'as usual'? Has Logan helped her with homework before?"

"You didn't know?" Patrick frowned. "Whenever you're out, those two are working. Either she's teaching him about hunting and fishing or he's helping her with school assignments."

Kyle blinked. *Huh.* He didn't know what to say what-so-fucking-ever.

Getting along with Logan and working together at the dock every day was proving to be harder than Kyle had anticipated, so he'd thought it was a genius idea to head out into nature when he had time off. Clearly, he hadn't considered all the things he'd be missing.

How come Lani hadn't mentioned anything?

"By the way, when you have time, could you drop off some whitefish for the dogs?" Patrick asked.

Slightly dazed, Kyle merely nodded. He finished the hare, gutting it and cutting up the meat, and then he walked outside to the temporary shed he'd built for the fish. They were strung on lines in several rows, perfectly frozen in this climate, and he collected a couple dozen of them. If he wasn't mistaken, there were twenty-four dogs on the grounds now, including Wolf and Kiery.

"Come on, buddy." He let out a whistle, and Wolf followed him toward the dog yard behind the backpackers' building.

Sarah was there, behind the fence, picking up shit.

"Hey, you." She smiled at him.

Kyle jerked his chin. "I come bearing fish."

"Oh, cool." It was her turn to whistle, and soon several dogs came tumbling out of their shed. "Justin, you in there?"

Kyle cocked a brow as he watched Logan's four-year-old leave the little building, too. Okay, *little* wasn't the right word. It was big enough to house over twenty dogs.

"I was playing with the puppies," he declared with a big grin. His nose and cheeks were flushed from the cold, but other than those and his eyes, he was hidden beneath layers of winter clothing. "Oooh, can I feed them, please?"

Kyle nodded and began sticking fish through the fence for him. Within seconds, the kid was surrounded by dogs with wagging tails.

It was kinda cute. Justin giggled madly as he threw out the fish for the Huskies to catch.

"Everything good with you?" Sarah asked.

"Huh?" Kyle faced her. "Oh—yeah. You?"

"Great." Her smile widened. "You've changed, you know."

"How so?" Kyle's gaze trailed back to Justin, a few more fish passing through the fence. Kyle also eyed a few of the pups, wondering if it was time to get started on the next phase of his life. He'd need more dogs for that, and he wasn't sure… It had always been a dream of his for Pinnuaq Bay—for the future. For "down the road."

"You're not as cocky anymore," she told him. "Or flirty."

He huffed a laugh. "Yeah, I guess." What else could he say? He knew he'd calmed down. Sometimes he wished he didn't give a fuck—like he never had before. Maybe he was growing up. At thirty-four, it was probably about damn time.

Sarah looked like she wanted to say something else, but Justin interrupted.

"Kyle?" he asked, wiping his nose. "Can I give a fish to Wuff too, please?"

"Sure." Kyle held up the last fish. "Through the fence?"

"No, I come out." He stumbled and ran over to the fenced gate and opened it. He carefully locked it from the outside, as Sarah had most likely taught him. "Here I am!" He grinned.

Kyle found himself grinning back at the tiny human. For a sniffling, unpredictable little kid, Justin Ward wasn't entirely bad. And that was saying a lot for Kyle, who got freaked out by children every time he saw them.

"Here, Wuff!" Justin happily waved the fish in front of Wolf. "Can I go to Daddy now?"

Kyle assumed Logan was in the staff house, so he automatically offered to take him. He was heading there, anyway.

"See ya at dinner." Kyle gave Sarah a two-finger wave before he followed Justin around the building.

"Hey, Kyle?" Sarah hollered.

Kyle stopped and looked over his shoulder.

"There might be a storm tomorrow," she said. "If it gets bad, Patrick said you guys would take tomorrow off, and he'd open the pool."

"Okay?" Kyle had no idea where she was going with this, and he wasn't comfortable letting Justin out of his sight. Well, he could still see the kid, but he wouldn't for long.

"Will, um…will you be there?" She fumbled with her words.

What's she been smoking?

"Probably." He frowned at her and then shrugged. Fuck if he knew what was wrong with her. Perhaps that time of the month. "I'm guessing we'll all be there in that case. We can talk about that later."

He took after Justin right before he lost sight of the little shit. Justin was like a bear cub, tumbling around more than running, albeit quickly.

"The snow's so deep here!" Justin laughed, digging his way through. Wolf jumped ahead with the fish in his mouth. "Wait for me, Wuff!"

It really was deep. The barbecue area that the three large buildings faced hadn't been shoveled, so the snow reached Justin's waist.

Kyle made a mental note to make a trail.

As always, Kyle kept an eye on his surroundings. The forest was quiet for now. They reached the staff house, and Kyle grabbed the long rope from a post by the steps to attach to Wolf's collar. If it got too windy, he could reach the doghouse a few yards away.

"He likes it outside," Justin said frankly.

"That's right. He's not like Kiery."

"Uncle Quinn says Kiery is his princess."

Kyle chuckled and kicked snow off his boots, causing Justin to mimic him.

"Does Wuff play with bears?" Justin asked as Kyle opened the door.

"Sure. Long enough for me to come help him defeat the bear with my rifle." This winter was particularly harsh, though. It was below fifteen most days, so it was no wonder Kyle hadn't seen any bears. They were probably all in hibernation.

"Whatsa dafeat?"

"Is that you, baby?" Logan called from the kitchen.

Nick of time. Kyle could only handle so many questions before he said the wrong thing and made the kid cry or something.

Unable to resist, Kyle answered Logan. "Yeah, it's me!"

Justin giggled and jumped in front of the doorway to the kitchen. "Hi! I need help, Daddy." He shook his butt and waved his mitten-covered hands.

"Goofball." Logan snickered. "Hold on, I'm just gonna wash my hands."

By now, Kyle was down to thermal pants and his hoodie, so he stepped around Justin to enter the kitchen.

Declan was setting the table for dinner, Logan was by the sink, Lani was both stirring something on the stove and reading from a schoolbook, and John was studying blueprints by the window.

"Hey, secret keepers." Kyle placed a freezing hand on Logan's neck, to which the man flinched and cursed. "*Miki*, what's this I hear about you and Logan doing homework and shit together?"

"It wasn't a secret." Lani scrunched her nose. "We're helping each other, and you're always out. Look!" She picked up a piece of paper and handed it to Kyle. It was an email from her teacher and test results. She must've printed it out.

"You got a B+?" Kyle was impressed. "Cool."

Lani smiled. "Thanks. Logan helped me."

Logan leaned close to Kyle while he was drying his hands and spoke under his breath. "Tell her you're proud." Then he walked out to assist Justin.

Kyle glanced up from the printout and saw Lani was back to stirring broth on the stove. He didn't know why, but he didn't brush off Logan's advice. Instead, Kyle walked over and dropped a kiss in Lani's hair.

"I'm proud of you. You know that, right?" He felt a bit out of place.

Lani's reaction made it worth any discomfort, though. Her smile grew tenfold, and she looked up at Kyle with surprise in her eyes. "Really?"

"Of course." Kyle was confused. Didn't Lani know that?

"*Sweet.*" Lani blushed and refocused on the food. "Maybe I can get an A next time."

"B+ is better than I ever got," Declan told her.

Kyle took a seat at the table, pondering what had just happened. He complimented Lani often enough, didn't he? Now he couldn't help but wonder if he was being too hard on her.

He was fucking clueless about this shit.

Logan evidently knew her enough to know what she needed to hear.

"Thanks!" Justin scrambled out of his thick snowsuit. "Can I watch a movie before dinner?"

"It's almost done." Logan hung up the clothes to dry. "You can go wash up instead."

"'Kay." Justin walked up the stairs, and Logan returned to the kitchen, his gaze seeking out Kyle's.

"How did you know?" Kyle mouthed.

"I'll tell you later," Logan replied in a hushed tone.

CHAPTER 8

Kyle looked forward to "later," but first it was dinner. Everyone filed into the staff house's kitchen for the meal Declan had cooked. Quinn arrived last, mentioning something about Valentine's day plans, and he smiled mischievously at Declan before taking his seat at the table.

It was a tight fit, and Kyle was squeezed in between Lani and Logan. Food was passed between them, and Kyle made an effort to pay Lani and Logan more attention.

Patrick appeared to be right. They were talking all throughout dinner. Lani wanted to take Logan fishing and hear the story about when he went to Ireland as a teenager. There was a "quiz" coming up, too. Lani was gonna show a bunch of illustrations of fish, and Logan was gonna name them by species.

They'd only been at the Retreat for a month. How had Logan and Lani gotten so close?

Was Kyle taking the distance thing too far?

"You're really serious about this, huh?" he asked Logan quietly.

Logan smirked faintly. "She's educating my Lower-48 ass. Like you said *you* would do."

All right. Maybe Kyle could stop avoiding Logan a little bit from now on.

"Kyle, do you think I could tag along when you go hunting sometime?" Sarah asked.

Declan's mouth twisted up. "The animal rights activist wants to go hunting?"

"You're one of those people?" Kyle made a face.

He carried only respect for people who were against trophy hunting, or those who fought for animals in captivity to be treated better; there were endless lists of things that were wrong. But too often, those people couldn't tell the difference between Japanese fishermen slaughtering pods of dolphins in cruel ways and a subsistence hunter who put food on the table for his family.

"I didn't say I wanted to *kill* the animals," Sarah muttered in her defense.

Kyle grinned and shook his head. She wouldn't kill the animal, yet she could eat it?

"I say this is an interesting development," Quinn said, smirking.

"I stand up for what I believe in." Sarah jutted out her chin. "I get that hunting in some aspects is okay—"

"Necessary," Kyle corrected. "We're not made of money, and as you know, this state isn't packed with grocery stores and ways to get there." This wasn't a debate he enjoyed getting into because it pissed him the *fuck* off. "Hunting is also how the Inuit have survived for thousands of years, so one might wonder what gives these hipster activists the right to claim they know better."

Sarah squirmed in her seat, though she wasn't about to back down. "We evolve. We realize there are some things that are wrong." She paused. "I...I understand like...hunting caribou and moose and other species we have so many of—plus, it's a clean shot, no cruelty—but that's different from, say, seal hunting." Kyle stiffened at that. "They shoot the seals first, except it's rarely a kill shot, so the seals suffer underwater until they can't hold their breaths anymore and have to resurface, only to be *stabbed* and reeled in by hunters."

Kyle struggled to keep his mouth shut. Sarah wouldn't

understand. Born and raised in California, only to have moved up here after college because of her passion for dogs.

"We don't want them to suffer. We kill the seals as fast as we can," Lani mumbled, picking at her food. "My elders say we're all on the food chain, seals and humans—everyone."

"Your family goes sealing?" Sarah flushed, seeming both shocked and embarrassed. Hopefully because she realized she'd put her foot in her mouth.

"Yes, ma'am." Lani nodded and reached for her juice. "We need the meat for food, blubber for oil, and pelts for clothes."

"You guys should've seen Lani's mom. Best seal hunter I ever saw." Kyle cut into his salmon. "Unfortunately, she and my brother died when a group of activists rammed their boat."

That sure ended the discussion.

The tension in the kitchen was palpable, and the silence couldn't have been more uncomfortable.

Kyle shoveled some food into his mouth, reminded of another reason for why he didn't like bigger cities and had no desire to see more of the Lower 48. Few understood his culture. Ignorance, he could handle. Ignorance could be treated by knowledge. But stupidity and judgment made him wanna punch a hole in a wall.

He visited New York once. Crazy place. He'd spent a week in LA, too. Even crazier. Montana and Washington were better.

Regardless, Kyle didn't judge how others lived. Didn't matter how outrageous he thought other lifestyles were; he understood everyone was different.

Somewhere along the road, it had become okay to find babysitters in video games, shut up kids with candy, and ease every ache with miracle drugs, but teaching a child how to provide for herself was *unthinkable*. Following traditions that were thousands of years old was *madness*.

"Excuse me." Sarah sniffled and hurried out of the kitchen and up the stairs.

Kyle lost his appetite. He was numb all of a sudden. Didn't feel a goddamn thing. He just stared at his plate and wished he were back in Barrow. Or his cabin in Pinnuaq Bay.

"I'm sorry, I don't know how to come back from that," Quinn said, widening his eyes.

That sort of worked.

Word by word, the others tried to leave the last ten minutes in the past, although Kyle stayed quiet. So did Lani, he noticed. Logan wasn't very talkative, either.

Once dinner was over, Kyle leaned close to Lani and asked if she wanted to watch a movie with him. She nodded, looking eager to get out of there, then said she had some more cooking to do with Logan for tomorrow first.

"Don't even think about it, darlin'." Logan reached over and squeezed her hand. "Declan's doin' the dishes, so I'm sure he can keep an eye on me and make sure I follow your instructions."

"I'll watch him like a hawk," Declan promised.

Lani smiled, and that was that. The two Shaws said thank you for dinner before going upstairs.

"My room or yours?" she asked.

"Yours," Kyle said. "You have the tablet."

They settled on the bed in Lani's room, and Kyle let her pick whatever she wanted to see. He didn't really care. He was only interested in relaxing with his niece for a bit.

"You okay, *miki*?" He lay back against the wooden headboard and beat his pillow into perfection. Then he held out his arm, and Lani got comfortable and drew up the covers.

"Yeah." Her finger traced the movie titles until she found some random comedy. "You made a girl cry."

Kyle hummed and kissed the top of her head. "Should I apologize?"

He found himself genuinely wondering. Because of what had happened to his brother and sister-in-law, he tended to have a short fuse when it came to the never-ending debate about hunting, so he couldn't be sure. He didn't think he'd done anything wrong, but maybe Lani knew better.

"I don't know…" Lani pondered. "Grandma Anyaa says an argument is not over until you part with a handshake, but Gramps says he would never shake the hand of someone who has judged him. It's very confusing. I'm only ten, Uncle Kyle."

"Sometimes I forget." He smiled into her hair before tilting his head to rest it on the pillow. "I'm just gonna close my eyes for a bit."

*

Logan yawned and stripped down to sweats. On his way to the bathroom across the hall, he grimaced and rubbed his neck—punishment for falling asleep at a weird angle while waiting for Justin to doze off. Eventually, the boy's sleep talk had roused Logan, and now it was close to midnight. The house was quiet and dark, except for two slivers of light underneath the doors to Lani's and Kyle's rooms.

After taking a leak, washing up, and brushing his teeth, Logan left the bathroom again, only to spy Lani tiptoeing out of her room.

Her hair was mussed up from sleep. "Hi. I'm gonna steal Uncle Kyle's bed."

"Why?" Logan laughed quietly.

"Because he's hogging mine, and he'll just be grouchy if I wake him up."

Logan deliberated for a beat and then asked, "Want me to be the punching bag? It's better he's a grouch with me than with you."

"I don't mind sleeping in his room for tonight." Lani waved it off.

But Logan couldn't let it go now. He'd barely seen Kyle this weekend, and tomorrow they'd be back at work again. "It's all right. I'll help you steal back your bed." He entered Lani's room and saw Kyle taking up most of her bed, one leg kicked out, an arm for a pillow, and his hoodie riding up to reveal his lower back.

Lani giggled behind her hands. "Get ready for some cursing."

CHAPTER 9

"Hey—sleeping beauty." Logan gently shook Kyle's shoulder. He was tempted to run his fingers through Kyle's silky black hair, though it would probably look weird.

He'd noticed how sexy and devastatingly handsome Kyle was from the first moment they'd met, but now...seeing Kyle like this, Logan added fucking beautiful to that list.

"Fuck off," Kyle grumbled. His eyes remained closed.

"No, *you* need to fuck off." Logan smirked. "You're in Lani's bed."

"She loves me. She can sleep in my room." Kyle turned toward the wall and buried his face in a pillow. "Go 'way before I stomp your fuckin' ass, Ward."

Lani let out another giggle, letting Kyle know she was here in the room.

Logan was a little distracted by Kyle's exposed midsection. Lying on his side, Kyle was putting all kinds of sexiness on display, from his ass dimples and some ink to the trail of hair that went south below his navel and his abs.

Physically unable to resist, Logan went for casual and placed a hand above Kyle's hip. "Come on, Kyle." Logan swallowed and flexed his fingers slightly, brushing over the soft skin.

Images of the two of them together flashed before his eyes, and there was more than desire. Something akin to yearning... In some way, he *missed* Kyle. Logan didn't even know how that was possible.

Kyle groaned and cursed and then stretched out along the bed as he rolled onto his back. It caused Logan's hand to shift so it rested on Kyle's lower stomach. *Fuck.* Logan's mouth went dry.

"*Qavsiñukpa?*" Kyle muttered drowsily and rubbed his face.

"Midnight," Lani answered.

"All right." Kyle grunted and propped himself up on his elbows. "You done feelin' me up, Logan?"

Logan's gaze shot to Kyle's face and was met by a lazy grin.

Logan felt his ears heating up, and he stood up abruptly. "Sorry." He knew he'd probably get his ass kicked if he went after Kyle again, but he couldn't fucking help it.

He wanted Kyle.

All of Logan's confusion regarding his sexuality didn't matter as much when labels and genders were removed from the equation, because it came down to the one person he couldn't stop thinking about. If that made him gay, bisexual, or pan-fucking-sexual, so be it.

He was gonna make a fool of himself and let his feelings show sooner or later, regardless of Kyle's reaction.

"Okay, I'm up." Kyle stifled a yawn and got out of the bed. "I'll wake you up bright and early tomorrow," he told Lani.

"Dark and early in this part of the world," Logan said, clearing his throat.

"Sleep tight, *miki.*" Kyle kissed the top of her head. "I'mma go nipple twist this motherfucker now." He jerked his thumb at Logan.

Lani laughed and jumped up on her bed. "G'night."

"Night, darlin'." Logan ducked out of the room and walked toward his own. He'd rather hide out in there now since Kyle had seen through his not-so-subtle way of getting his hands on Kyle.

"Not so fast, Ward."

Damn. Logan paused by his door and turned to Kyle. "What?"

Kyle took his time, closing Lani's door and then walking over. "I was serious." He closed the distance and actually twisted Logan's nipple. "That's for waking me up."

Logan hissed and rubbed his nipple. "What the fuck, dude?"

Kyle shrugged and grinned. "Anyway. Now that I've got you alone, mind explaining what happened earlier with Lani? The pride thing. She lit up like the sun."

It was Logan's turn to shrug. "She needs to hear it every now and then. It's not a big deal—you're great at praisin' her, but you're pretty much her entire world. Hearin' you're proud of her means a lot."

Kyle folded his arms over his chest and looked down, a crease forming between his brows. "I've never thought of it that way. It's weird."

"What is?" Logan leaned his shoulder against the door.

"Being someone's world."

Logan could relate. Before Justin, he'd never had anyone depend on him, either. "It's both cool and scary as fuck." He cocked his head, curious about the nickname Kyle had for Lani. "What does *miki* mean? You always call Lani that."

"Means 'little' in Iñupiaq." Kyle's mouth tugged up. "She was the tiniest little shit when she was born. I almost dropped her once, so my brother dragged me outside and clocked me in the jaw."

Logan chuckled. "I would've loved to see that. Was he your younger or older brother?"

"Older." Kyle dipped his chin. "He was born to be that girl's dad. Me...not so much. Kids freak me out."

Logan *had* noticed that Kyle got uncomfortable around Justin, but Logan wouldn't go so far as to say it was bad. It was just... Kyle spoke to kids the way he spoke to adults.

"Speaking of your brother—well, sorta." Logan coughed quietly into his fist. "About before, with Sarah. I didn't know that was how they died. And Sarah criticizing the way you live only made me feel like more of a shit for lashing out on you the first day we were here."

"It's all right." Kyle smiled wryly. "At least you're doing something about it. Everyone's entitled to their own opinion—the only thing I ask is that people try to understand before they preach."

"Maybe Sarah will try to understand now, too."

"Maybe." Kyle didn't look like he believed it. "Anyway, play your cards right and I just might take you hunting."

Logan huffed a chuckle. "Not sure I'm there yet. Going to the shooting range at home for shits and giggles is one thing, but I doubt I'd be useful in the wild where the targets are moving."

"All in good time, my man." Kyle offered a quick grin. "At least now I know you can actually fire a gun. Makes me hot thinking about it." With a wink, he turned and headed for his room. "Goodnight, Ward."

"Night, asshole." Logan sighed and shook his head in amusement. "By the way, would you even survive in Florida? If the tables were turned, I mean." Kyle paused and looked at Logan over his shoulder. "Would you melt?"

Instead of showing mirth at the joke, Kyle only observed Logan.

It got to the point where Logan regretted asking. He didn't even know why he'd done it.

In the end, Kyle flashed the beginning of a smile. "Who could say no to palm trees and half-naked beachgoers? I'm sure my ass could be surgically removed from Alaska if a Florida local wanted to show me around. Goodnight."

Logan was left alone in the hallway, and his mind started filling up with images of what it would be like to show Kyle around Florida.

It felt...strange.

*

"Well, this is depressing," Patrick muttered into his coffee mug the next morning.

Kyle grunted in agreement and took a sip from his own mug. They were both standing by the window in the kitchen, looking out at another whiteout.

Had the dock been closer, they would've been able to do

interior work today. It was the matter of getting there that was the issue. With almost zero visibility, icy winds, heavy snowfall, and a temperature of almost forty below, it might as well have been Barrow.

Kyle had gotten up at seven as usual, taken one look out the window, and decided not to wake up Lani. And as soon as Patrick had confirmed there'd be no work today, John and Alex had returned to their rooms. Sarah had avoided eye contact, bundled up, and braved the storm to tend to the dogs.

"Has Logan been down yet?" Kyle wondered.

"Yep." Patrick nodded, still staring out the window. "Justin wakes him up around six every morning, so it's usually the three of us for the first cup of coffee."

"Jesus." Kyle couldn't imagine being forced out of bed because a kid didn't wanna sleep anymore.

"It's not that bad," Patrick chuckled. "If the Retreat had been closer to civilization, Nina and I probably would've had a couple by now."

"You love this place too much, or…?"

Patrick shrugged one shoulder. "I think so. It's supposed to be secluded. It's home." He paused and looked down at his coffee. "We've played with the idea of opening our home to older kids, though. Maybe younger teenagers who need to get away from bad influences or broken homes."

Sounded like a fine idea to Kyle. One didn't have to travel far to run into kids who needed the support, and Patrick and Nina were good people.

The sound of someone coming down the stairs brought the conversation to a halt, and Kyle turned to see Logan entering the kitchen.

He looked irritated and tired. "Justin fell back asleep. Of-fucking-course, no matter how much I tried, I couldn't do the same."

"You poor thing." Patrick snickered and sat down at the table. Kyle followed suit. "I wonder if Dec and Quinn are snowed in." He glanced out the window, pensive.

"Kiery will have to go out sooner or later." Kyle stretched his arms above his head and yawned. "Oh, about that." He straightened and faced Patrick as Logan joined them with his own mug. "Any plans for the newest pups?"

"Not really," Patrick replied. "When it's the busiest here, we need enough for three sled teams, and we have that." He nodded at Kyle. "You have any of the pups in mind?"

Kyle inclined his head, half hesitant, half eager. "I'm not sure I'm ready to go all out yet, but if you have two of them for sale, I'll buy. Are they related to Lola's litter?" Breeding came to mind for the future.

"No, we brought in a male from a buddy in Nome, and Lola's not the mother this time." Patrick leaned forward a bit. "Are you starting your own sled team or something?"

Kyle grinned faintly and shook his head. He wasn't ready to divulge, but that wasn't it. "It's more of a security matter and retirement policy."

Logan chuckled. "You're what, thirty-three, thirty-four?"

"Thirty-four, and it's not too soon to start planning," Kyle answered with an easy smile.

"Well, you go ahead and pick out two," Patrick said and stood up. "Don't even think about paying." He went over to refill his coffee. "I'm saving money on you, Shaw."

"You're paying me to both work and bring home meat," Kyle said with a frown.

Patrick shrugged. "That's how expensive it is to fly in food otherwise." Huh. Kyle thought about that for a minute. Patrick went on. "I would've started hunting myself if I'd had the time. At least to bring down the costs for me and Nina, but..."

Kyle could do something about that. "If you get the permits, I can come down here every now and then and stock up the cache. It could cover plenty for you and the staff."

"I'll definitely consider that," Patrick said. "Thanks, man. I'm gonna go upstairs and call my wife. Dec should be up soon, too."

Then there were two.

Kyle side-eyed Logan, knowing there were two roads he could take. Option one: continue the distance—which he both hated and doubted he could manage for much longer—and maintain a friendship. Kyle would see Logan when he ventured up from Florida to visit Quinn and Declan. Maybe an online message or text here and there.

Option two: get close and hope for another roll in the sack that the sexy construction worker would most likely regret the next day, and then break all contact when Logan flew home again.

Option three only existed in fantasy, and Kyle locked and threw away the key to that little place in the back of his head.

"Any plans for today?" Logan asked, leaning back in his seat.

Kyle admired the defined muscles hiding underneath Logan's formfitting T-shirt. "I don't know yet," he murmured. "I have two pups to pick out. Other than that..." He shrugged slightly and scratched his elbow. "Might go for a swim. Patrick's gonna open up the main house. What about you?"

"I'm on kitchen duty, but Lani and I have already prepared everythin'," Logan answered, yawning. "I wouldn't mind sleepin' away the day, and I know just how much shut-eye I can get if the pool's open. Justin loves the water."

"As much as he loves snow?" Kyle grinned.

Logan chuckled. "It might be a tie." Scooting forward a bit, he reached over to grab the bowl of sugar. Their knees bumped together under the table, and Logan didn't move away once he'd poured some sugar into his coffee. "It might be a tie for me, too. Never saw that comin'."

Kyle eased forward as well and rested his forearms on the table. "What, snow and water?"

He preferred not to think about it—because it could get his hopes up—but that didn't mean he'd forgotten that Logan had said it didn't really matter where he ended up. Florida or Alaska. As long as Logan could find stability.

"Okay, maybe not the snow," Logan amended. "The state in general. And after two years of teasing Quinn about moving here, I have a whole lot of shit to eat if I settle down in Anchorage or something." He smiled, stirring the coffee with a spoon. "I do think it's way too fucking cold, but the nature's stunning. The little I've seen of Anchorage is great, too."

Option three rattled in its box in Kyle's head, and he pushed that down. He wasn't about to let his loneliness dream up scenarios that were too goddamn out there. If Logan did settle down in Alaska—great. Fucking awesome. They'd be able to get together for dinner and hang out with Quinn and Declan whenever Kyle found himself in the city.

"Do you know the best way to get hooked on the Alaskan winter?" Kyle asked.

"No?" Logan looked to him, curious.

Kyle smirked. "Spend a summer here."

"That doesn't make any sense."

"It will," Kyle said confidently. "The endless days are cool and all, but the mosquitoes will make you dream of snow."

Logan's shoulders shook with laughter. "We have mosquitoes in Florida too, you know."

"Not like ours." Kyle sorta hoped he would be there to see Logan's face when he saw Alaska's mosquito swarms blacken the sky. If Logan chose to live here, that was. "We have *jokes* about the mosquitoes here."

"Do tell, Shaw." Logan grinned. "I need a sample."

Kyle racked his brain and then snapped his fingers. "Okay, I've got one. Our mosquitoes are so big they gotta alert air traffic control before they lift off."

Logan cracked up and shook his head. "It's like Alaska's version of Yo Mama jokes."

"It really is." Kyle hadn't thought about it like that. He laughed and tried to remember other jokes, only to up empty. Probably because it was too early in the morning.

"Daddy!" Justin called from upstairs.

"Already?" Logan groaned. "I love that child more than anythin', but *Christ.*" He scowled at Kyle's chuckle. Then he rose with a sigh and walked out of the kitchen, pausing at the foot of the staircase. "What have we said about yelling, Justin? The others are sleepin'."

Kyle looked over his shoulder and checked out Logan's ass in those sweats for a bit. He also admired how daddy-like Logan was. He reminded Kyle a lot of his big brother, who could stomp and whine about never getting enough sleep, but then he'd be putty in

Lani's hand.

"I peed," Justin told Logan.

Kyle withheld a laugh and watched as Logan hung his head and put his hands on his hips.

"Where?" Logan asked carefully.

"In the toilet."

"Oh." Logan definitely brightened at that. "That's great, baby. Did you wash your hands?"

Little feet ran away.

Logan turned to Kyle with a tired smile and said, "I might as well make sure he doesn't turn the bathroom into a war zone."

"Have fun." Kyle smirked.

CHAPTER 10

To Logan, a quick getaway to the pool wasn't so quick. Almost everyone at the Retreat was planning on spending the day in the main house, so first, Logan had to pack all the food. Then he had to locate trunks and floaties and new clothes to change in to later. Lastly, he had to get Justin dressed in several layers and his thick snowsuit, topped off with face mask, extra scarf, beanie, and mittens. In the meantime, Justin was asking when they were gonna go, when they were gonna go, when they were gonna *goooo*.

That wasn't even the worst part.

From door to door, it was only some fifty feet, but when one added three feet of snow, winds out of this world, more snow coming down, and an impatient four-year-old, it wasn't a fucking walk in the park.

When Logan opened one of the double doors to the main house, he let out a huge breath of relief.

The lobby of the main house was pretty cool. High ceiling, a fireplace roaring with life, animal hides on the walls, a friggin' moose head, wooden beams across the ceiling with a chandelier made of antlers in the middle, big sofas, rugs, and a front desk... He could see why Nina and Patrick loved their business.

In the middle of the rustic floor was a wood post with several arrow-shaped signs. Some showed the direction of the pool, spa, and restaurant, and some showed the distance to locations like Mt. Everest, Yellowstone, the Everglades, the Sahara, and the North Pole.

"Can we go swimming now?" Justin grunted and fell back on his butt as he tried to take off all his snow-covered layers. "My mitten's stuck, Daddy!"

Logan chuckled, too amused to let his frustrations win, and helped his son. "It's a good thing you're so damn cute."

"Nana says I look like you."

"And isn't Daddy cute?" Logan squatted down to unzip Justin's snowsuit.

Justin giggled and nodded, scratching a finger across Logan's beard.

"The cutest," he heard a voice say behind him. *Quinn.*

Logan looked over to see Quinn and Declan coming up from the basement where the pool was. They had clearly been in the water already and were now only wearing trunks with towels around their necks.

"Hey." Logan grinned. "Who else is here?" He only knew that Patrick had gone with Kyle to the dogs so he could pick out his pups. Lani was there, too.

Quinn used the corner of his towel to wipe some water drops off his face. "John and Alex are downstairs, and Sarah's in the attic reading."

Logan glanced at the signs. "Isn't that the spa?"

"It is," Declan replied. "But it's mainly an open space with a skylight. Many guests go up there when the lights are out." The little smirk he shot Quinn told Logan what else they could do up there.

Quinn flushed and wiped his face some more, probably to cover up. "Anyway...we're looking forward to lunch."

Subtle. Logan laughed as finally got Justin out of his winter layers. "And I'm looking forward to seeing those *lights* you've bragged so much about, Quinn."

So far, Logan's experience with the Northern Lights was meh.

There'd been a green fog-like light a couple nights. Nothing spectacular like in Quinn's photos.

Declan and Patrick said it was because of the weather. They were having an unreasonably harsh winter with very few clear days. Or nights, rather.

*

By the time Lani and Kyle made it to the main house, he was the owner of two new pups. A black and white male with crystal blue eyes named Scout, and a white little bitch Lani named Isa. Short for *isagulik*, it meant angel.

"Are you gonna let the puppies be with Wolf?" Lani asked as they entered the lobby of the building.

"Eventually." Kyle nodded and pushed down his snow pants. "They're only three months old, so they're not big enough to spend the nights outside yet. But I'll take them out of the pack so they can spend a few hours with Wolf every day."

"Maybe it's best they sleep in my room," Lani said solemnly.

Kyle laughed. "I'm sure you think so. We'll see." He hung up his jacket and grabbed his bag with their swimwear. "Come on, let's see what the others are up to."

They headed downstairs and soon followed the sounds of Justin's squeals.

When they reached the humid pool area, Kyle saw Quinn and Logan tossing the four-year-old between them in the water, and Logan was hot as hell in nothing but black board shorts clinging low to his hips. His tan looked golden in the dim light, and the water trickling down his toned torso was making Kyle's mouth go dry.

John and Declan were sitting at one of the two picnic tables by the short end of the pool playing cards, and Alex had his head in a magazine.

"Hi, Lani!" Justin called out, waving enthusiastically.

"I'll go change." Lani looked excited, and she walked briskly toward the dividers at the other end of the pool. "I'll come in soon, Justin!"

Declan looked up from his game and smiled. "You don't happen to have my brother with you, do you?"

"He'll be here soon. He had some calls to make," Kyle replied. With a glance Logan's way, he said he'd go change, too. *Damn*, that man was fine.

"Actually, we were just waiting for you guys—it's time for lunch." Logan swam closer to the edge with Justin. "I'll go get the food, and we can eat down here as soon as Patrick comes."

"And Sarah," John added with a smirk.

"She's still avoiding everyone." Quinn moved toward the edge, as well. "I can go up and ask her, but I'm pretty sure she'll wanna eat up there."

Kyle knew he had to talk to the woman. *Later.* So while everybody scattered, he went to change. And Lani got twenty minutes of pool time before they were all gathered—not including Sarah—for lunch.

Kyle ended up at a picnic table with Logan, Declan, and John. Justin had wanted to sit with Quinn and Lani, so they were at the other table with Alex and Patrick.

"Here's to Lani helpin' Logan make somethin' that's actually edible," Quinn toasted, holding up his glass of soda.

Logan flipped him off, though he was grinning, too.

Kyle snickered and dug in to his food, which really was good. Pan-fried halibut, fresh sandwich bread, gravy, and carrots that had been in the oven with lots of butter.

"I think it's time I show Quinn the pool is my domain." Logan spoke quietly so the others at Quinn's table didn't hear. "What do you guys say about a little competition?"

"I'd say Quinn needs it," Kyle chuckled quietly. "I've tried countless times. The fucker always beats me." It stung a bit, he had to admit. "You sure you can take him?"

Logan merely laughed and faced Declan and John to hear what they thought.

"I do like a friendly bet every now and then." John smirked.

Declan sighed. "Well, I'm obligated to bet on my fiancé, so…"

"What're you guys whispering about over there?" Alex asked,

his eyes narrowed in suspicion.

"*Nothing*," Logan insisted.

*

Logan and the others spent the next couple of hours tiring out the kids with volleyball and playing tag. Justin was high on life and marshmallows, but it was only a matter of time before he was yawning more than giggling.

Gotta love naptime.

Lani wanted to watch a movie and she had homework too, so the timing was perfect. Logan carried Justin upstairs to the lobby and the couches there, dried him off, and bundled him up in soft blankets. In the meantime, Kyle added wood to the fireplace and helped Lani set up her tablet.

"Rules?" Kyle asked Lani.

She dutifully recited each one. "I won't leave him alone, we won't leave the lobby unless we're coming down to the pool—together—I'll holler if I need anything and also when he wakes up."

"I'm not tired, I promi…" The rest of Justin's sentence went unheard as he fell asleep.

Logan smiled and kissed the top of Lani's head. "You're amazin', darlin'. Thank you. He always sleeps a little over an hour, so I'll come up and check on you guys."

When Logan looked over at him, Kyle wore a strange smile.

On their way back down to the pool, Logan asked him about it.

"You don't treat Lani any differently than the way you are with your garden gnome," Kyle answered pensively.

Logan didn't really know what to make of that. *Garden gnome?* And had he crossed some sort of line? He enjoyed spending time with Lani; they learned a lot from each other, and the little girl was a total sweetheart.

"For fuck's—" Kyle cut himself off just as they reached the doorway to the pool, and Logan looked up.

He frowned, confused, not seeing anything out of place.

Declan, Patrick, and Quinn were in the water, John and Alex were chatting at a table, and Sarah...*Sarah*.

Sarah was sitting on the edge of the pool, and her bikini was barely there. White, fucking tiny, exposing most of her slender body.

Logan eyed the other men and now noticed some of them were throwing her subtle glances. Quinn appeared amused. Declan looked skeptical. Alex and Patrick were casually admiring a sexy woman just like they would with Hollywood actresses on TV. John seemed to be on the same page as Quinn.

None of that mattered, though. At the sight of Kyle's flushed cheeks, Logan almost felt sick. Sick with raging fucking jealousy.

Yeah, she was attractive, Logan guessed, but this wasn't how it was supposed to go, goddammit.

I'm a fucking idiot, he thought bitterly and walked over to a plastic chair in the corner. While he'd started hoping for more, mustering courage to pursue Kyle again, he'd clearly moved on. Or maybe there was nothing to move on from.

Logan clenched his jaw and dropped the towel on the chair, and then he walked over to the pool and dove in.

CHAPTER 11

Kyle was pissed.

Scratch that. He was furious.

He'd been looking forward to some downtime without the kids, and now he had to deal with Sarah. Wasn't it enough that the pool area was already crowded as it was? Fucking hell, he wished they could all disappear—not counting Logan. Obviously.

Lunch had been cool—same with the couple hours that had followed. Kyle felt closer to Logan lately, and he didn't want the day to get ruined by being reminded of the issue with Sarah. That could wait. Kyle wasn't ready to talk, anyway. At least not like a civilized person.

Fuck this. He was gonna enjoy this day with his buddies. He'd just pretend Sarah wasn't here, and if she approached and wanted to talk, he could tell her there was plenty of time for that later.

Following Logan's lead, Kyle headed into the water, and he stayed submerged until his lungs burned. He broke through the surface a few feet away from Declan and Patrick.

"I don't know. Quinn might be on to something," Patrick was saying, keeping his voice down.

"About what?" Kyle scrubbed his hands over his face and

then pushed back his hair.

Declan hummed, eyeing Quinn—who was speaking quietly to Logan in the middle of the pool—and then turned to Kyle with a little smirk. "Seems there's a new bet going on." Kyle raised a brow, and Declan chuckled and shook his head. "It's entirely possible we're too bored around here if we end up taking bets based on *gossip*, but Quinn believes Sarah's after the guy she shot down two years ago."

Kyle grimaced. "Quinn's out of his mind. And yeah, definitely bored. Last time I checked, we weren't high school girls." Irritated with the mention of Sarah, Kyle swam over to Logan and Quinn. "Hey." He poked Logan's side. "Maybe it's time to do what you talked about during lunch."

Kyle needed the distraction.

Logan grinned and slid his gaze to Quinn. "What a coincidence. I was just tellin' Quinn about it."

Quinn didn't look happy. "I'm the fucking champ."

"Then you won't mind taking on Ward here." Kyle draped an arm lazily around Logan's shoulders. "If it makes you feel any better, my money's on you, Quinn."

"What the fuck?" Logan's eyes snapped to Kyle.

Kyle stifled his amusement and shrugged. "I've seen how fast Quinn is. I haven't seen you."

It didn't matter how fast Logan was, regardless. Kyle had a plan, and Logan's confidence had made most of the guys think he was better than Quinn. Kyle would simply use the odds to work in his favor. Declan had succeeded once upon a time. Now it was Kyle's turn.

"Fine," Quinn grumbled. "Let's get this over with." He swam away and told everyone he was gonna race Logan.

Of course, the other guys were quick to gamble.

Only Declan and Kyle put down money on Quinn.

"I'm insulted, Shaw." Logan shook his head. "I figured since you've had your cock up my ass, I'd at least get your vote."

Kyle's eyes went large, and he glanced around to make sure no one had heard that. *He* didn't give a shit, but Logan did.

Didn't he?

"Did you forget?" Logan faced Kyle fully and tilted his head. He inched closer, too. "Huh? Is your head filled with thoughts about Sarah's tits, or do you remember that we fucked in Anchorage?"

There was so much wrong with that sentence, Kyle didn't know where to begin.

He narrowed his eyes, about to ask what Logan was talking about, when Quinn hollered for Logan to quit stalling.

That gave Kyle pause. He held Logan's stare for a bit longer and then said, "Get the fucking race over with. Then talk to me in plain English."

His head was full of what-the-fucks as he swam over to the far end of the pool. He was the only one there, and he watched absently while Logan and Quinn got into position. Patrick stepped up to do the countdown, and when he called to Kyle and asked what he was doing all the way over there, Kyle responded that he was gonna see who touched the wall first—in case they were evenly matched.

Bullshit, but whatever. He wasn't gonna reveal his plan.

Pushing himself out of the water, he sat down on the edge, one leg on either side of the line that divided the two lanes. His eyes zeroed in on Logan, and his mind couldn't stop spinning.

What about Sarah's rack?

Kyle glanced over at Sarah, who was now at the picnic table. She looked out of place, nose in a book she was struggling to read. The pages never turned.

Two years ago, Kyle would've hit that. He also would've fucked any random person on the street. It was how he'd lived for years. Eternal bachelor. The idea of settling down was always farfetched.

Now, though? *Fuck my life*, Kyle sighed internally. The only motherfucker he saw was Logan. During the short time they'd known each other, he'd gotten under Kyle's skin.

"Ready...set..." Patrick let out a sharp whistle, and the Florida guys were off.

Shoving away his thoughts for now, Kyle slipped into the water again—in Logan's lane—and waited.

They both looked like professional swimmers, cutting through the water with practiced techniques and strength. Logan was faster. Not by a lot, but enough.

Halfway into the race, Logan had some five feet on Quinn.

"Come on, Ward!" Alex clapped.

Mirth trickled into Kyle. 'Cause this was fun. He steeled himself and waded out a couple feet in the waist-deep water, and by the time the others were shouting at him to get out of the way, Logan was too close.

Kyle leaned forward and tensed his body, and the impact came a second later. Logan swam straight into Kyle, effectively blocked from reaching the wall and winning.

"Goddammit!" Logan growled. Water drops ran down his face, and he shot Kyle a glare as he tried to shove past. However, that was when Quinn finished the race. "What the hell, Kyle!"

As soon as Quinn saw what was going on, he started guffawing. "Looks like I win!"

Kyle smirked, and he called over to a chuckling Declan. "Collect our money, boss!"

Quinn got up from the water to walk back to the rest, a triumphant grin on his face.

"Oh, come on!" Logan threw out his arms. "There's no way that counts. We gotta do it again—without *this* dumbass blockin' my way!"

"Such language." Kyle tsked and twisted Logan's nipple.

"What the…" Logan appeared torn between anger and wanting to laugh. "That's fucking it." He threw himself at Kyle and grabbed him in a headlock.

Right before Logan dunked them underwater, Kyle sucked in a quick breath and screwed his eyes shut. The sound of laughter was drowned out beneath the surface, and he struggled to contain his own laughs while he dodged Logan's fingers trying to dig into Kyle's sides.

He managed to push himself up but was soon backed into the wall by Logan.

Kyle could probably get away if he wanted to, and he didn't. He wanted to see what Logan would do.

"You're gonna regret that, Shaw," Logan threatened with a dark smile. "All I'll say is sleep with one eye open."

"I'm shaking in my boots," Kyle drawled. Straightening, he stood face-to-face with Logan, and fuck if he was gonna back down. With no more than a sliver of air between them, Kyle's mind took a nose-dive to the gutter. "Does that mean you're gonna visit my room at night?" He looked Logan up and down, inexplicably drawn to the masculinity of his torso. Defined pecs hid underneath a dusting of chest hair. An even tan made the shadows of his abs more visible.

"Would you reject me if I did?" Logan's low voice had grown husky.

Kyle cleared his throat, goose bumps spreading across his body. "No…" He lifted his gaze from Logan's chest. "But I'd kick your ass all the way back to Florida if you regretted it the morning after."

"That's fair." Logan took another step, causing their bodies to touch. "It was never about regret, though."

Try telling Kyle's bruised ego that, though he knew the truth in the back of his mind. He knew it'd been too much for Logan— at that time. And now?

"Do you know what you're doing?" Kyle felt hands settle on his hips, Logan's thumbs drawing mindless circles over Kyle's skin. Jesus Christ, his heart was threatening to pound its way through his ribcage. "It's awfully public for you, isn't it?"

"Shut up, Kyle." With a tilt of his head, Logan brushed his lips to Kyle's, quick to apply some pressure.

Kyle went with it. He didn't wanna think about afterward; he'd deal. Somehow. Now was more important. Logan's lips were soft and warm, so goddamn inviting. Closing his eyes, Kyle angled his face to deepen the kiss, and Logan let out a quiet groan and parted his lips.

"*Whoa.*" That was Alex.

"Holy shit." Quinn.

The taste and feel of Logan's tongue drove Kyle mad with lust, but the kiss remained unhurried and sensual. Gripping Logan's hips, Kyle pulled him closer and let his hands trace the lower part of Logan's back.

Logan's beard scratched Kyle's face gently whenever they shifted, a big contrast to the softness of Logan's mouth. Kyle was hooked. He was hard as a fucking rock too, and so was Logan.

Logan was an intoxicating kisser, and Kyle wouldn't have complained if they got locked inside here for the whole damn day.

"Jesus," Logan muttered, out of breath. His fingers ghosted up along Kyle's arms. "Do you want me to wine you and dine you, or can we find some privacy soon?"

Kyle chuckled huskily and swept the tip of his tongue across Logan's bottom lip. "Lucky for you, I don't drink wine and I'm not hungry." At least not for food. "I gotta make sure you know what you want, though."

He liked Logan. A shitload. Feelings were developing, and Kyle didn't wanna be discarded like yesterday's paper once their time at the Retreat was over.

"I want *you*." Logan took charge for a beat and kissed him so hard it left Kyle's lips tingling and his lungs burning for air. "Fuck, I can't control it anymore—can't hold back."

A shiver ran down Kyle's spine. He didn't even know Logan *had* tried to hold back. Relief and satisfaction coursed through Kyle, and even though he didn't know yet where they stood—was this casual or...?—he decided to deal with that at another time.

"Okay." Kyle slowed the kiss and reached up to gently cup Logan's jaw. "Fucking hell, you know how to kiss." He pushed his tongue into Logan's mouth, groaning quietly. "I guess we have a firing squad to face, but tonight... Soon as the kids're asleep."

Logan nodded quickly, breathing heavily. His eyes were dark with desire, and Kyle fucking loved it.

Then he reluctantly dragged his gaze away from Logan and looked toward the other end of the pool. Kyle would've loved to have seen that nobody was there. Sarah wasn't, but the other guys were waiting. Only Declan, John, and Patrick had the decency of appearing busy with a card game. Quinn and Alex wore expectant expressions.

"Talk about outing yourself, Ward." Kyle dropped a kiss to Logan's neck before inching away. "You just made the cover of

Retreat Daily."

"I don't care." Logan sank into the water and started a languid swim toward the other side of the pool, and he looked back to make sure Kyle followed. "I'm done complicating things."

"What do you mean?"

"Labels and shit." Logan turned around so he was floating through the water backward. "I guess I thought I'd feel better once I figured out my sexuality, but the information out there fucked me up."

Kyle grinned faintly and stepped in between Logan's legs, pulling him closer. "Sounds like someone turned to the internet."

"Briefly." Logan sighed and leaned in. Under the surface, they were almost completely wrapped around each other. Only their heads and shoulders were visible to others. "I don't even know what sapiosexual means."

"And now you don't care?" Kyle's arms circled Logan's middle, his fingers playing absently with the waistband of Logan's trunks.

"No." Logan nuzzled Kyle's jaw and dropped a kiss there. "Guess it boils down to the person for me, and lately there's only one."

Christ, something sure had changed. "The blonde we fucked?" Kyle hummed, enjoying the light teasing. He was also basking in this new...openness, he guessed he could call it.

Logan chuckled quietly and shook his head no.

Lowering his head, Kyle leaned close and tasted the skin of Logan's shoulder with an openmouthed kiss.

"Hey, guys?" Evidently, Quinn was growing impatient. "If you could just get the fuck over here and answer some of my questions, I'll babysit for the rest of the day."

Kyle and Logan were quick to face each other.

Logan could probably see what Kyle wanted 'cause he answered fast. "Deal."

*

To Logan, it was like a fog had been lifted.

Most of Quinn's questions went unanswered; there was still a whole lot Logan didn't know, yet he felt more at peace than ever.

"How long has this been goin' on?"

"Is it serious?"

"Why did Sarah storm out lookin' all pissy?"

"Did somethin' happen in Anchorage?"

"Logan, does this mean you're movin' to Alaska?"

"It's new," Kyle had grunted in response to the first question. Then they'd both shot Quinn a frustrated look at the second. *"Fuck if I know,"* Kyle had said and shrugged at the third, although Logan sure as shit knew. Sarah wanted Kyle, Logan was sure of it. *"None of your business"* wasn't the answer Quinn had wanted to the fourth question, but it was an answer nonetheless. Logan was still reeling from the jealousy, so he hadn't been able to be nicer about it.

Logan knew the difference between curiosity and genuinely needing to know, though. The only question Quinn had really cared about was the last one, and Logan had been honest.

Yeah. I'm probably moving.

He hadn't looked at Kyle while answering. It was too soon and felt more than a little presumptuous. Nevertheless, Logan liked Alaska; Justin fucking loved it. That was enough to consider the move seriously, and a shot with Kyle sweetened the deal.

Hell had officially frozen over, and as Logan and Kyle got dressed and headed back to the staff house—leaving children and babysitters behind—images of finding an apartment in Anchorage popped into Logan's head.

Maybe he'd live close to Quinn and Declan. They could all go out together now and then with John and Alex and their families. Perhaps Justin would become friends with Alex's youngest. Maybe Logan could become a dog owner, too.

Holy shit, he was fucking *excited.*

He didn't know where Kyle would fit in to all of this, yet for the first time in ages, Logan was hopeful. And the second they were out of the raging storm, he pounced. Right there, in the middle of the hallway in the staff house, he shoved Kyle up against a wall and kissed him hard.

Kyle let out a groaned *oomph* before he caught on. Jackets, boots, and beanies were thrown in every direction as their hands grabbed and pulled.

"My bed," Kyle grunted into the kiss.

"Yeah." Logan pushed his fingers into Kyle's hair. Tilting his head, he deepened the kiss and began walking backward in the direction of the stairs. "Fuck, I want you." Kyle tasted amazing. Mint and swimming pool and marshmallows. "This fuckin' body…"

Kyle growled and reached to unbuckle Logan's belt. "Move faster." They never broke their sloppy, bruising kiss.

Stumbling up the stairs, they shed clothes on the way and nothing had ever turned Logan on more than Kyle. His kisses were drugging, his hands were rough, his voice was like whiskey, and his entire masculinity made Logan's cock throb.

He felt Kyle's long fingers brush over his trimmed beard, Kyle's touch both gentle and demanding.

"Don't ever shave this off." Kyle's husky whisper caused Logan to shudder, and as soon as they reached the landing, it was his turn to be pressed up against the wall. Kyle had him caged, and he leaned in and swept his tongue into Logan's mouth.

Logan dipped his chin and nuzzled Kyle's neck, inhaling deeply. Another few steps were taken toward Kyle's room.

"I wanna taste you," Logan admitted, his teeth scraping over Kyle's jaw. "Feel your fingers in me—oh, Christ." He let out a moan as Kyle palmed his cock. Logan's pants were pooling by his feet, so it was only his boxer briefs in the way.

"And what about this?" Kyle fisted Logan's cock and gave it a slow stroke outside the fabric. "You wanna fuck me with this thick cock before you take me in your mouth?"

"Fuck, yes," Logan groaned, his mind going wild. "*Please.*"

CHAPTER 12

Kyle finally pushed Logan into his room, all while warring with himself about protection. Oh, he *had* it. But fuck, he wanted feel the wetness of Logan's tongue on his skin. Kyle wanted to slowly slide his cock into that mouth and feel it all.

"Are we safe?" he murmured into a kiss. "I won't take any risks."

"I'm clean." Logan pulled his T-shirt over his head and then tugged at Kyle's wife-beater. "I've been tested since a broken rubber gave me Justin."

It was too tempting for Kyle. "I'm clean, too." He got rid of his beater and pushed down his pants and boxers. "Get on the bed." With all their clothes gone, Kyle stroked himself and got the lube out of the nightstand drawer. "It's been a while for me, so go slow."

Once he joined him on the bed, Kyle thought Logan would get right to it. He was wrong. Logan covered his body and drove him mad with passionate kisses. He explored Kyle's body with skilled fingers.

Logan kissed his way down to Kyle's chest, lips closing over a tight nipple. Kyle hissed and bucked his hips. At the same time,

Logan gave the head of Kyle's cock a sensual twist and stroked him downward.

"Jesus," Kyle muttered. He was fucking trapped in a haze of desire. "Here." He handed the bottle of lube to Logan.

Logan sat back between Kyle's legs. For a moment, he only stared at Kyle's body—eyes dark and showing hunger—while he stroked himself. Then he slicked up a few fingers with a generous amount of lube and lowered his face to Kyle's crotch.

While he carefully pushed one finger inside, he took the tip of Kyle's cock into his mouth.

"Oh fuck," Kyle groaned. His hand came to rest at the back of Logan's head, his fingers brushing over the short, dark strands.

Logan let out a quiet moan, closed his eyes, and took more of Kyle's cock.

Gritting his teeth, Kyle's head fell back against the pillow, and he let the pleasure take over. A greedy mouth on his dick and two fingers fucking him—goddamn glorious. Then a third digit was added, and he was suddenly desperate to feel Logan inside him.

"Now." Kyle nudged Logan away from his cock, only to grasp it and jack it quickly a few times. "Fuck me."

Logan applied lube to his erection and crawled up Kyle's body, fast to claim his mouth in a deep kiss.

"Goddamn sexy." Logan placed a wet kiss behind Kyle's ear. "You taste better than I do."

Kyle cursed and shuddered, imagining Logan tasting himself. "Doubtful." He palmed Logan's perfect ass, feeling a slicked-up cock sliding between his thighs. "Is that a habit? Tasting your come?"

"Every now and then." Logan hummed and peered down between them as he guided his cock to Kyle's hole. "Only since I discovered jerkin' off."

"Fuck." Kyle had the urge to say that should be his job now, swallowing Logan.

At an excruciatingly slow pace, Logan inched deeper and deeper inside, and Kyle had never felt so full. A dull burn flared up, causing his cock to soften slightly, but the immense desire remained. Logan was everywhere. Physical pleasure, Kyle was the master of. He was experienced. He knew how to get someone off. He just hadn't known there could be more to it.

"Holy shit." Buried all the way in, Logan dropped his forehead to Kyle's shoulder and breathed shallowly. "Too fuckin' good."

"Move—I need more." Kyle tilted his head and pulled Logan in for a kiss. The pain was fading, and need was building up rapidly in Kyle's body. "God, Logan…" He moaned into Logan's mouth as the man began moving.

They touched every inch they could reach. Strokes, kisses, nips, and caresses. But that only lasted for so long. As the minutes ticked by, slow and careful was replaced by rough and dirty.

Sparks of burning pleasure shot through Kyle in a blinding rage as Logan rammed into him. They groaned and smashed their lips together, tongues mingling and teeth sinking into soft flesh.

"This isn't a one-time thing, Shaw." Logan slid out then pushed in again, a growl rumbling in his chest. "I won't get enough."

Kyle's chest expanded, relief and the approach of his orgasm nearly making him delirious. "Me either." He controlled the kiss and met every thrust, and it only got worse when Logan gripped his cock firmly and jacked it. "Shit, I'm getting close."

"Good," Logan panted through a groan. "I'm about to lose it." Swiping his thumb over the head of Kyle's cock, Logan smeared pre-come all over, mixing it with the lube. "Hottest fuckin' sight…"

Kyle realized they were both looking down between them. At Logan's hand working Kyle's cock expertly. At Logan's cock pushing in and out of Kyle's ass at the same pace. At their defined abs flexing with every movement.

Unable to hold back a second longer, a drawn-out groan escaped Kyle and he lolled his head back against the pillow. His hands fisted the sheets as ecstasy exploded in his gut, radiating outward. Kyle felt the orgasm everywhere. The tips of his fingers, his toes, his spine. Stream after stream spurted out of his cock, and Logan held his hand over the head and rubbed it in, his strokes slowing down.

Then Logan cursed and started coming, too. He buried his face in the crook of Kyle's neck, sucked in a quick breath, and rocked into Kyle's ass a few more times before stilling.

Mind: completely blown. Kyle couldn't form a single thought.

Logan squeezed Kyle to him, both breathing heavily. Eventually, Logan drew back and collapsed next to Kyle.

"We gotta do that again," Logan muttered drowsily. "I had a plan and all."

Right. He'd wanted Kyle's cock releasing in his mouth.

Kyle chuckled lazily and turned, nuzzling Logan's jaw. "There's always next time."

It felt fucking good to be able to say that.

"I want you to fuck me, too." Logan yawned and slid a leg up Kyle's hip. "Damn, I could get used to this."

Me, too. Kyle hummed and pressed his lips to Logan's forehead.

Kyle heard his phone buzzing somewhere, but that could wait. He was much more interested in round two with Logan.

*

After hours in bed with Kyle, Logan stumbled out of the room to get something for them to eat. Kyle was still napping, and Logan wanted to get back as fast as possible.

He tightened the drawstrings of a pair of Kyle's sweats he'd found on a chair and looked down to see sleep lines on his exposed chest. Had his hair been longer, it would've been disheveled as fuck. Kyle's was.

Logan winced when he took the first step down the stairs. *Okay, careful it is.* He'd certainly gotten what he'd asked for, and now he was sore. It was fucking hot. If this continued, he might turn into Kyle's very own bottom boy. Obscenely dirty murmurs, a hard cock, and then an out-of-this-world blow job had nearly made Logan forget his own name.

As he entered the kitchen and opened the fridge, Logan could hear they weren't alone in the house. A shower was running somewhere above him, music was coming from one of the many rooms, and there was a fresh pot of coffee on the counter.

He found some leftovers and popped the first plate in the microwave. The storm had calmed down, and Logan looked out the window while he waited for the food.

It was dark by now, but a porch light behind the building across the yard lit up the snow enough to reveal Declan and Kiery. He was throwing a ball for her, which she had to jump through several feet of snow to dig out.

Logan grinned when he saw Quinn and Justin appearing from the cabin that was just out of view at this angle.

Lani wasn't far behind.

Logan made a mental note to thank Quinn and Declan again for watching the kids later.

"Nice sweatpants."

Logan turned around, spotting Sarah entering the kitchen with a vacant smile. Peering down, he got that it was *Barrow Whalers* written across the pant leg that bugged her, but there could be two reasons. Either she was jealous that Logan had—literally—gotten into Kyle's pants. Or…she was taking the Whalers thing all wrong. It wasn't about hunting. Logan had learned from Lani it was the name of Barrow's high school football team.

He didn't know what to say, so he said nothing. Instead, he waited for the microwave to ding, and then he replaced the plate with the other one and pushed two minutes.

The smell of caribou, steamed vegetables, and mashed potatoes made Logan's stomach snarl. The gravy on the side was sizzling, so maybe he'd overdone it.

Sarah sat down at the table with a cup of coffee. "Is it serious between you two?"

Logan knew he didn't owe her any answers. He wanted to. He wanted to be honest and say what had been building up in his mind for weeks now.

"It is for me." He checked the microwave. It hadn't even been a minute.

"Kyle's changed a lot in the past couple of years," Sarah mused. "He used to be this womanizer—well, he went after guys, too. He hit on both me and Quinn the first year."

"Uh-huh." Logan had no idea why she was saying this. He really didn't give a fuck about their pasts. Quinn was an attractive guy, so why wouldn't Kyle have noticed that? As for Sarah...yeah, she was attractive, as well.

"I like him now," Sarah admitted.

"I know." Logan did know. He'd noticed. "I got jealous." He had no issue admitting that. At first, when Sarah had walked into the pool area in that skimpy bikini, Logan was sure it was lust he'd seen in Kyle's expression. But after that, Logan had seen Kyle throw enough scowls and glares in her direction to ease Logan's fears.

"Wait, was that why you went after him?" Jesus Christ, Sarah's tone of voice actually held *hope*. "Because you don't want him with me?"

Logan let out a quiet snort, his eyes never trailing away from the microwave. "Sorry to disappoint, but no. You're not the only one who likes him."

He might have moved faster because of Sarah's appearance in barely nothing, except that was only a matter of days. Logan's mind had been made up before. Hell, he was fucking falling for the man.

"What's it to you, anyway?" He couldn't help it. He narrowed his eyes at her. "Do you think being against his entire culture is the way to win him over?"

Sarah cringed and looked down at her coffee. "Hunting's not all there is to Kyle. I feel bad for arguing with him about it, but we could work it out."

Was she nuts? She was talking as if a relationship between her and Kyle was a done deal simply because she "liked him now."

Logan shook his head and turned back to the microwave. *Almost done.* "I hate to break it to you, but as long as you don't know the difference between hunting for profit and what he and his family do, you won't even be on his radar. Thinking a pair of tits is enough... Ain't that a little insulting?"

"Excuse me?" Sarah spluttered. "Who are you to preach when you're against what he does, too?"

A dark chuckle slipped through his lips, and he removed the plate from the microwave. It was hot as hell, so he set it down on the counter. "I don't know where you got that from. It's a load of shit." He'd made a big mistake when he judged Kyle for taking Lani out to hunt, but that was before Logan knew better. He'd gotten it all wrong because his views on guns had been shaped by city-living and war zones. It was different here. Guns had a different purpose here. "I admire him—and Lani—for everything. While most people are used to just drivin' to the store to put food on the table, they go out and find it themselves."

With that said, Logan put the food and utensils on a tray, grabbed a couple beers, and aimed for the stairs.

Then he came to an abrupt halt when he looked up at the stairs and saw Kyle sitting on the landing.

Damn. How much had he heard? Logan couldn't be sure, and Kyle's face gave nothing away.

What Logan had said to Sarah was nothing he'd hide from Kyle though, so he didn't stall. Then when he got to the final steps, Kyle didn't move. Instead, while blocking the way, he leaned forward and slid his hands up the backsides of Logan's thighs.

Logan lifted the tray to look down. "You okay?"

Kyle nodded and pulled Logan closer, humming as he pressed his face into Logan's crotch. "You look good in my clothes."

Logan's mouth tugged up. Shifting the tray to one hand, he freed one to weave his fingers through Kyle's hair. "How about some food?"

Another nod from Kyle. "Yeah." He kissed and groped Logan through the soft fabric of the sweats a few more times then stood up. "By the way?" On his first step toward his room, he looked at Logan over his shoulder and smiled. "I'm serious about this, too."

Logan grinned back. So Kyle had heard everything. And it was fine. More than fine.

*

Kyle didn't know how hungry he was until he'd settled against the headboard and had a plate of leftovers in his lap. It looked really good, which meant Logan hadn't cooked it. *Cool.*

The plate was too hot since he was only wearing boxers, so he yanked up the covers and set the plate on top of that instead. "Is this from Alex's dinner the other day?"

"Yeah." Logan shoveled some food into his mouth and then bumped his shoulder to Kyle's. "So...you have nothin' to say about what you heard downstairs?"

Nothing Kyle was ready to admit out loud until he knew more about where they'd go from here. But yeah, hearing Logan defending him—*understanding* him—was pretty much the final nail in the coffin. Logan was the man who now had the ability to make or break Kyle.

"I liked what I heard," he offered. "Except for Sarah's bullshit."

Learning that Sarah wanted him?

Oh, the fucking irony.

"She would've made a decent distraction two years ago," Kyle went on, gathering some meat and mashed potatoes on his fork. "Guess I have higher standards now."

What Sarah had said to Quinn downstairs had also made Kyle change his mind about talking to her. There was no way they'd solve anything, so Kyle had dodged that one.

"I'm flattered," Logan chuckled.

Kyle angled his head and dipped down to bite Logan's shoulder. "You should be. I'm awesome."

Logan merely smiled and shrugged, as if saying "No argument from me," and then handed over a bottle of beer. "Somethin' to wash down Rudolph the reindeer?"

Kyle snorted a laugh at the joke, though he declined the beer. "You keep that one. You'll need the sugar if you wanna keep up with me tonight."

Logan's eyes flashed with lust, though a pensive expression won out as he popped open the beer and took a swig. "I've never seen you drink alcohol."

"That would be correct." Kyle chewed what was in his mouth and went for more. "I've never touched the stuff."

"Nothing alcoholic whatsoever?" Logan turned to him and blinked in surprise. "Not even *beer*?"

Kyle smirked and shook his head no, his mouth full of food.

Once he'd swallowed, he said, "Never saw the point."

People who noticed he never drank always expected some dramatic background. Like alcoholism, an accident, or illness. Over the years, many had thrown out guesses: Did you lose someone in a hit-and-run? Are you a recovering alcoholic?

The answer was no.

"Huh." Logan sat back, stumped. "No other reason?"

"Not really." Kyle scratched an eyebrow. "I mean, from the moment I knew what alcohol could do, I decided to stay away from it. And it wasn't anything dramatic—nobody died or got into trouble." He remembered a party from his high school days; older friends or family members had imported drinks, and teenagers getting giggly and ridiculous was like going to the zoo for Kyle. He'd stared at his peers all night, wondering what the fuck was so appealing. "It was weird." He shrugged. "And some talk about liquid courage—it makes you braver. To do what, things you're not really ready for?"

"Damn." Logan let out a strained chuckle. "I definitely went for liquid courage in Anchorage. Without it, I wouldn't have gone into the guest room that night."

"And you weren't ready for it," Kyle pointed out.

Logan bobbed his head and turned, dropping a quick kiss to Kyle's shoulder. "Does it bother you, though? Others drinkin', I mean."

"Of course not." Kyle smiled. "Considering I've never had it, I would be hypocritical if I judged others for doing it."

"Touché." Logan smirked.

They ate in silence for a moment, and Kyle could hear people coming in from outside. Muffled voices. Children's laughter. Their gnome-free day was over, but for some reason, Kyle wasn't annoyed by it. He'd half expected to be.

"I'm ready now—you know that, right?" Logan asked.

Kyle knew, and he fucking loved it. "Screwing me sober and telling me it wasn't a one-time thing kinda tipped me off." He winked and then reached over to leave his empty plate on the nightstand. "So how are we on sneaking into each others' bedrooms at night?" He leaned in and kissed Logan's neck while his hand traveled under the covers. Right under Logan's plate. "Would Justin mind if I stole his daddy while he sleeps?"

Fucking hell, how could Kyle already want more? They were both gonna be sore and aching all over tomorrow as it was.

"No…" Logan cleared his throat and moved his plate away from there. Then he pushed the covers aside so he could see Kyle rubbing his junk. "He definitely won't mind. As long as we can leave the doors ajar afterward."

Kyle could work with that. "I wanna fuck you again."

Logan was quick to straddle Kyle and kiss him fiercely.

A quickie couldn't hurt.

CHAPTER 13

"Daddy?"

Logan hummed, half-asleep, and tightened his hold on Kyle. It was so fucking warm and cozy under the covers, and spooning Kyle had turned him into a goddamn cuddler. For the past few weeks, whenever they woke up together, someone was always holding the other.

"He's sleeping, cub," Kyle murmured in his morning voice. "What's up?"

Logan had his back to the wall, Kyle in front of him, so when he squinted, he could see Justin standing next to the bed. His hair was all over the place, his pajamas rumpled.

"My fort is gone," Justin said.

Logan hid his grin behind Kyle.

The fort had been Quinn fuckin' Sawyer's idea.

Lani's curious glances had been replaced by blushes and eye-rolls and embarrassed giggles whenever Logan and Kyle were affectionate toward each other in public, but Justin hadn't even cared. He also hadn't cared when Logan had asked what he thought about Daddy sleeping in Kyle's room at night.

Then Quinn had piped up and said, *"You know what, kiddo?*

This is where you say it's only okay if Kyle and Daddy build you a fort first. You gotta know how to play 'em."

"*Yeah, okay,*" Justin had laughed.

So Logan and Kyle had spent that evening turning the bed in Logan's room into a fort. Four posts held up blankets to shield the bed from the outside world, and there was a password to get in.

"Did you pull down one of the blankets in your sleep again?" Kyle asked, sounding both tired and amused.

"Yeah," Justin replied sheepishly. "I need to pee."

"That's your cue, *piv*." Kyle reached behind him and placed a hand on Logan's hip. He shook it a little. "Wake up. Your tiny human needs you."

"I'm up," Logan answered drowsily. Lifting his head, he saw the clock on the nightstand flashing six AM. Normal time to wake up for his son. "You won't tell me what *piv* means... Can you tell me why you're calling Justin cub?"

Piv, whatever it meant, was new. Kyle had called Logan that for the first time the day before yesterday, and when Logan asked what it stood for, he'd only gotten a grin and a head-shake in return.

He figured it was something in the Inuit language, so he'd asked Lani, but she was tight-lipped about it, as well. Tight-lipped and rosy-cheeked.

"Because he's like a cub," Kyle said, as if it was obvious. "He rolls around and stumbles in the snow more than he walks and runs."

"I like snow," Justin laughed.

"No shit." There was a grin in Kyle's voice.

His boy started doing the pee-pee dance, so Logan got a move on. He climbed over Kyle and gave him a quick peck before he ushered Justin out of the room. With the occasional nightly visitor, Logan and Kyle always slept in sweats, so any emergency toilet break was dealt with swiftly.

"I'm hungry," Justin announced as he flushed the toilet.

Logan pointed to the sink as a silent reminder, and Justin went to wash his hands. "I'm sure Uncle Patrick has somethin' ready in the kitchen already."

Seemed like everyone had become "Uncle" to Justin and Lani, and Logan felt more at home every time he heard the guys referring to themselves as that. It was suddenly more than friends he'd found up here. It was family.

How could Logan wanna leave that?

He and Quinn Skyped with Quinn's parents every now and then—Justin too, of course—and they could tell Logan was sold. Pam had complained because now she'd lose another "son" and, to boot, her only grandson.

Quinn had retorted with, *"Guess you'll just have to come up and visit a lot."* He was smug as hell because his mission had been completed. Logan and Justin would be Alaska residents soon.

The only question was where they'd settle down.

It was no secret to anybody that Kyle disliked cities, so Logan was still unsure about that.

As they left the bathroom, Justin held up his arms, and Logan didn't deny him. It was so rare that Justin wanted to be carried these days that Logan reveled in it when it happened.

He picked Justin up with a little grunt and positioned him on his hip. "You're gettin' big, baby." He placed a smooch on Justin's forehead. "I love you."

"Love you," he said, squishing Logan's cheeks together.

Walking down the stairs, they joined Patrick in the kitchen—the other early riser at the Retreat. He was sitting at the end of the table, radio playing quietly in the window. By now, he was probably on his second cup of coffee, and he had to be running out of his precious Sudoku puzzles.

"Mornin'." Patrick looked up briefly and smiled and then returned to his puzzle. "Pancakes on the counter for the little one."

No matter how many times Logan had told him he didn't have to make breakfast for Justin…

"Thank you, man." Logan let Justin down to have a seat. "What do you say, Justin?"

"Thank you, Uncle Patrick," Justin said with a grin.

Logan ruffled his hair before walking over to the counter.

"You're welcome, champ," Patrick replied.

To everyone's surprise, Kyle entered the kitchen then. He

always went back to sleep for another hour after Justin had woken up Logan.

"I gotta call my dad soon," was Kyle's explanation. He slid in next to Justin at the table and yawned as he placed his cell phone in front of him. "Stubborn old bastard."

Logan poured them coffee and reheated two pancakes for Justin. "Was it today he had his doctor's appointment in Fairbanks?"

The day after Logan and Kyle had gotten together, Kyle had spoken to his neighbor up in Barrow. Kyle's father wasn't resting as instructed, and his recovery from his hip surgery wasn't going well. The neighbor had called to basically rat out Kyle's dad, so now Kyle was on the warpath. He checked in with his pops often, and Logan had heard him yelling at his father more than once. But it seemed both Shaws were stubborn as hell.

"Yeah." Kyle scrubbed his hands over his face tiredly. "Worst case scenario, I gotta fly out for a couple days and make sure he picks up his meds before going home again." He grimaced. "Fucking hate Fairbanks. And worse than regular doctors? *Specialists*. Always so damn arrogant."

Logan chuckled under his breath and brought the food and beverages to the table. Kyle nodded in thanks, and Justin poured syrup on his pancakes until Logan said that was enough.

"Well, let me know if there's anythin' I can do," he told Kyle.

"Can I sit on your lap?" Justin asked Kyle, and without waiting for a response, he crawled up onto Kyle's lap.

Logan stifled a laugh at the comical expression on Kyle's face at the same time as he sort of loved his view across the table. It did things to him whenever he saw Kyle and Justin interacting.

"I, uh…I think we've discussed this, cub," Kyle told Justin. "I'm not comfortable with humans your size. You're untrustworthy in terms of voicing your needs, and I'm horrible at guessing. You're also like a knick-knack or a figurine—you break easily, and I'm like a bull in a china shop."

Logan and Patrick exchanged highly amused glances.

Kyle wasn't done. "Plus, your dad won't be happy if I accidentally make you cry or some shit, not to fucking mention, I'll have a heart attack. Can you sense a pattern? It's all going downhill from there."

Justin was nodding along while he chewed on his syrupy pancake—as if he understood a single word of what Kyle was saying.

As for Logan, he was fairly sure he fell in love with Kyle that very moment. Or rather, realized he had fallen.

Kyle could preach all day long about not liking kids, except that wasn't the case whatsoever. He just didn't know how to act around them.

If he genuinely didn't like children, Kyle wouldn't be protective. He wouldn't go out of his way to shovel a path across the yard so Justin could walk easier. He sure as hell wouldn't be caught napping with the kid, and he wouldn't so naturally take Justin into consideration when they worked over out by the dock. Before the weekend, he'd even told Patrick when it was time to head back because Justin had been tired, cranky, and cold.

"You're still sitting on my lap," Kyle pointed out to Justin.

Justin giggled, shoved some more pancake into his mouth, and nodded.

Taking pity on the man, Logan offered to take Justin, but Kyle huffed and rolled his eyes and said it was fine.

It was more than fine, and Logan was gonna make sure Kyle knew how great he really was with Justin.

*

Kyle was mildly irritated by the fact that he gave a shit about the boy in his lap. It would've been easier without feelings sometimes. Instead, he was stuck caring about someone who also terrified him. Fucking hell, he was useless with Justin. The kid sometimes told his daddy he needed to go to the bathroom approximately two and a half seconds before he...*went*.

He was also a liar.

Justin claimed he wasn't tired when he was fucking exhausted.

What the fuck was Kyle supposed to make of *that*? He relied on people telling him what he needed to do.

He was screwed. He'd gone and fucked himself over by falling for a man who had an ankle biter. And they were both good people, too. Logan was pretty much everything Kyle wanted in a partner, and Justin was eager to learn new things. The kid wasn't delusional. They'd seen a fox lurking around the dock the other day, and rather than gushing about how cute it was, Justin kept his distance and asked if it was dangerous.

Kyle stared at Justin as he finished his breakfast, feeling something stirring in his chest. *Fucking feelings.* Then he was saved by his phone, so Kyle excused himself to go upstairs and take the call.

He saw it was Roger, their neighbor, so he sat down on the bed and answered. "I was just gonna call Dad. Is he up?"

There was a beat of silence before Roger replied. "I think you need to come home, son."

Kyle blew out a frustrated breath, picturing his dad pitching a fit about going to Fairbanks today. "Look, he needs to go. If something's wrong, it won't heal well and he can kiss his boat goodbye because he won't be able to stand on his own—"

"He's dead, Kyle."

Kyle blanched. Those were words he couldn't process. His dad was fucking fine. He was only fifty-eight, for fuck's sake. He had years of fishing and hunting left once he'd recovered from breaking his hip. Roger was goddamn crazy.

"Are you there?" Roger asked carefully. Maybe Kyle made a noise 'cause Roger went on. "I went in to wake him up so he wouldn't miss his flight." There was a pause. "He must've died in his sleep, Kyle. The ambulance just picked him up."

Kyle didn't know what to say. His mouth wouldn't form words. His body was running cold and he could feel despair gripping his heart, but there was nothing else. His brain had shut down.

"I'm very sorry, son. Do you want me to arrange flights for you and Ilannaq?"

Oh, fuck. Lani.

Panic rose in Kyle, and he was the first one to admit he didn't know how the fuck to deal with this. Lani was gonna be devastated.

"I'll take care of it," he rasped.

He ended the call and stared unseeingly at the phone in his lap, not really comprehending what was going on. Dad was fine a couple days ago. Moody and bored, but fine.

Now he was...dead?

"Kyle?"

Kyle lifted his head, wondering why it was like lifting a boulder, and saw Logan in the doorway with a concerned look on his face.

"My dad died," Kyle said numbly.

"What?" Logan's eyes grew wide, and he crossed the space with a few quick steps. "Are you serious?" He sat down next to Kyle.

Kyle nodded jerkily. "Last night. Maybe it was a stroke...? Fuck if I know."

"Jesus Christ." Logan pulled Kyle close and kissed the side of his head. "I'm sorry, sweetheart. What can I do?"

"Nothing." Kyle relaxed into the hug and closed his eyes. For two goddamn seconds, he wanted to forget about everything and just be with Logan. "I gotta go home."

Logan continued dropping soft kisses to Kyle's head. "I know," he murmured. "Do you know how long—" He sighed. "Never mind. I'll ask my questions at a better time." He pressed his nose in Kyle's hair and inhaled. "I'll miss you. Focus on Lani and yourself and call me when you can."

Kyle hummed in acknowledgment. "I should talk to Patrick." While they were done with the exterior of the buildings by the dock, they still had a lot to do inside the two lodges. Kyle being the electrician here, he was needed. But his work could also be postponed and done later. "I don't know if I'll be back before the time is up here."

They only had a little over a month left, and Kyle had no idea how much time he needed at home. He refused to think of any kind of burial, and there was more than that. Paperwork, Dad's business, dealing with family...

"We'll work it out."

Kyle needed more than that—solid plans of when he'd see

Logan again. Hell, even the cub. A specific date to look forward to.

*

Only seven hours later, Logan stood by the airstrip and watched Mitch's plane land in the darkness.

Lani was inconsolable. Kyle was…distant.

Everyone was in shock over what had happened today, though all Logan could focus on was Kyle's impassive expression. He sat on a crate full of gear and looked out at nothing. Wolf was next to him, watching the two new pups—Scout and Isa—wrestle with their own leashes.

"Hey." Logan squatted down in front of Lani. "You can call me whenever you want. Day or night. Okay?"

She sniffled and nodded.

"I'll call you, too." He removed a glove and wiped some tears away from her cheeks. "I'm gonna miss you so much, but we'll see each other soon, all right?"

"Yeah," she croaked. She threw her arms around Logan's neck. "I love you."

Logan's heart both soared and broke. "I love you too, darlin'." His eyes burned, but dammit if he was gonna let emotions get the best of him. He'd be strong for the two people he'd come to love as much as he loved his own son. "Can you make me a promise?"

Lani nodded. "What?"

"If your uncle gets too quiet and closes himself in, promise you'll let me know right away." Logan brushed away more tears from her beautiful face. "Justin and I will be on the first flight if you need us. Okay?"

"Okay."

"Good." He kissed her on the forehead, and in his periphery, he saw Justin shuffle closer. "Wanna give Lani a hug, baby?" He eased away.

Justin both shrugged and nodded. He didn't understand the concept of death yet. He just didn't like that Kyle and Lani were leaving.

"Bye, Lani," he mumbled, wrapping his arms around Lani's

middle.

Lani hugged him back, and Logan walked over to Kyle as Mitch got out of the plane.

The three of them loaded the luggage in silence, and then Kyle helped Lani and the dogs get seated in the plane, strapping them in safely. The others at the Retreat had already said goodbye, so they stood back when all was done, giving Kyle and Logan some privacy outside Mitch's plane.

"I told Lani I'll be on the next flight with Justin if you need us," Logan said, pressing his forehead to Kyle's. "I mean it."

Kyle didn't respond verbally, but he kissed Logan long and hard, his silver gray eyes glassy with unshed tears when he broke away.

And before long, Logan was watching the plane lift off with what felt like half his heart.

Christ.

Sighing heavily, Logan turned and headed back to where the others were waiting. Though, by now it was only Declan, Quinn, and Justin left.

"How're you doing?" Declan squeezed Logan's shoulder.

"Better than the Shaws." Logan shrugged and picked up Justin. "I wish there was more I could do."

"I have a feeling you're already doin' more than you think, buddy." Quinn smiled sympathetically. "You took care of everything today."

Arranging flights and helping Kyle pack wasn't enough, in Logan's opinion. Had he not had obligations here, he would've gone with Kyle and Lani right now.

"Hey, how about we have a couple beers at our place?" Declan suggested. He winked at Justin. "And maybe a hot chocolate for the...what is it Kyle calls him?"

Unable to stop it, Logan's mouth twisted up slightly. "Everythin' from knick-knack and tiny human to garden gnome and cub."

"Garden gnome?" Quinn cracked up.

Declan chuckled. "I was referring to cub, but the others are certainly...colorful."

Logan smiled, though it faltered fast. It pained him too much to think about happier times that included Kyle, so he changed the topic altogether. On the way to Declan and Quinn's cabin, he got them to talk about their wedding instead. Hawaii this summer. Just the two of them. Then they'd visit Sarasota for a dinner with Quinn's folks. Then a party in Anchorage when they returned. Logan was invited to either or both, depending on where he settled down, Declan told him.

Quinn threw an arm around Logan's shoulders and said Alaska was home to Logan now.

Logan agreed.

CHAPTER 14

A week later, Logan didn't feel as settled as he had lately, though. He was only getting sporadic texts from Kyle. Logan had learned that Kyle's dad had died from a heart attack, and Logan was surprised to also find out that Lani was staying with her grandmother on her mom's side for a bit. It worried Logan because he knew Kyle and Lani needed each other.

Feeling uprooted once more had caused Logan to make a rash decision two days ago, although he didn't regret it. If anything, it was the only thing that held him in one place now.

Patrick and Declan had been discussing further expansions for the Retreat while they were working by the dock, and Logan had been listening in. Money was a little tight, but if Patrick could find cheap labor, they'd be able to host summer camps for preteens in the hostel-like building and add their own hiking trail with shelters for camping along the way.

Declan was on board but disliked the idea of cheap labor.

"Give me a cabin, and I'll work for free four months out of the year," Logan had blurted out. Everyone had gone quiet and stared at him. Then Quinn's wide smile made Logan go on. And think on his feet. *"Whether it's for construction or helping out in general—four months of*

free labor a year and regular pay for whenever else you need me. Help me with hunting permits too, and I'll learn how to pitch in with food." He wanted to learn anyway, and he knew it'd bring down costs.

"Deal," Patrick had said, grinning.

Tomorrow was Saturday, and Logan was gonna spend the day moving his belongings from the staff house to his new home. He'd also surprise Justin and tell him to go pick out a puppy for them.

Logan was ready to adapt and learn everything he could about living up here. The only reason he hadn't offered the entire year was because Justin would need to spend time with his own peers, too. Maybe Logan would move to Anchorage and split his time like Declan and Quinn did; he wasn't sure. School wasn't something he had to think about yet, and later there was always long-distance schooling. But for the social interaction aspect, Justin would need more than this. Plus...Kyle. Logan wanted them together.

So far, they'd have the three dead months since Kyle was a permanent fixture here for the coldest part of winter. Now, Logan would just have to find a way to add more months to that count.

If only Kyle would pick up his phone. Random texts that said *"We're hanging in there. Miss you"* and *"Sorry I missed your call. I was working"* didn't ease Logan's worries.

*

Kyle was running on fumes.

After five days way out in the Beaufort Sea, he was able to pay off the entire crew, and Dad's boat had a new owner. Once they'd docked, Kyle threw his duffle over his shoulder, pocketed his profit, and grabbed a crate of fish he'd kept for himself then began his journey back to Barrow on his snowmachine.

Out there on the frozen tundra, Kyle had always been at ease. *Usually.* The area was breathtakingly beautiful, but it didn't do shit for Kyle anymore. The lights were out tonight; neon blue and green splashed across the sky, and it became even more picturesque when Kyle drove near a roaming polar bear. Yet, his thoughts were with Logan, Lani, and Justin.

It had been nearly two weeks since Kyle's dad had passed, and the fog of depression hadn't lifted. In fact, it had gotten worse, but he had so fucking much to do.

Dad's affairs were all but finished though, so Kyle hoped to find peace soon.

When he reached Barrow, the first stop was at Lani's grandmother's house where his dogs were staying temporarily, too. Lani was withdrawn and quiet, which only depressed Kyle further. He couldn't take care of her right now, as much as he wanted to. Soon, hopefully. For now, he was buried in work and obligations.

"Stay for some *maktaaq*, boy." Anyaa waved him into the kitchen.

Kyle dutifully got up from the couch in the small living room, except he wouldn't leave without Lani. He held out his hand.

"I have homework," she mumbled.

"I don't give a fuck. Sit with us in the kitchen for a bit and pretend you missed me."

Lani glared up at him, though the glare was soon replaced by sadness. Tears welled up in her eyes. "I wanna come home, Uncle Kyle."

Kyle swallowed hard. "Me, too. But I gotta head out again soon." He'd promised to take Lani's aunt's twin boys on a week-long hunt ages ago—when they first returned from their college years in the Lower 48. They wanted Kyle's advice and some more experience before they became providers of their own. Especially Joakim, who'd returned with a wife.

It was how they did it up here. They passed on the knowledge and helped out.

"Have you talked to Logan?" Lani asked.

Kyle hesitated then shook his head. "We've texted a little…" That was all on him, because if he heard Logan's voice right now, Kyle would fucking break.

"He's worried about you," Lani said.

"I don't have forever, boy!" Anyaa called from the kitchen.

Kyle winced. "All right. Come on." He held out his hand again.

Lani was a stubborn girl, though. She raised a brow. "If you shut people out, you can damn well go eat with *Aaka* Anyaa alone,

112

too."

Kyle deserved that, so he had no choice but to face the elder of the family on his own. Well, one of the elders. The most inquisitive one. Some people called her wise, too...

He'd barely sat down before she started. She might be frail-looking, only two shits high, wrinkled, and white-haired, but she had balls. She sorta had to, considering she'd raised four boys and two girls, the youngest being Lani's mom.

"Your home is not in Barrow no more." She took her seat across from him and slid a plate of *maktaaq* to the middle of the table. "If your home is not in Barrow, your work is not in Barrow."

"Cryptic." Kyle picked up a piece of frozen whale meat and cut off the blubber. He'd never really liked it.

"Akh!" Anyaa made a face. "You not eatin' it right."

Kyle gave her a flat stare before he stuck the morsel into his mouth and chewed. Without fucking blubber.

Anyaa sighed and muttered something in her language—maybe Yup'ik. Kyle could rarely tell which one it was. Their family came from all over the Arctic, and Anyaa spoke more than one language and several dialects.

"It is time to move on, boy," she told him wisely. "You belong in Pinnuaq Bay. And I am reluctant to admit—so does Ilannaq. You have prepared for a life there since you were only seventeen. It is time, Kyle."

*

"Pull!"

The clay pigeon was shot into the air, and Logan fired Declan's shotgun.

Hit.

"Yay, Daddy!" Justin's voice was muffled by the protective headphones they were all wearing.

Logan found out trapshooting worked great for someone with anger issues, and he had a lot of those these days.

Three weeks. It had been three goddamn weeks since Kyle and Lani left, and Logan was fed up. He spoke to Lani almost every day after work. Kyle, not even once.

"Pull!"

He fired.

Miss.

He'd gotten pissed the first time a week and a half ago, and Patrick had introduced him to trapshooting. So now, whenever he had time off and the weather permitted it, he drove out with Patrick or Declan and Justin to open grounds and shot the anger out of his system, however temporary it was.

"Pull!"

Hit.

"Good job, Ward," Declan said. They paused while he stocked up the machine with clay disks. "It's not even been two weeks. Either you're a natural or you went to the practice ranges in Florida a whole lot more than you let on."

Or maybe he was just that pissed off.

"I used to go with Quinn and one of his uncles back in the day." Logan grabbed his thermos and refilled his coffee mug. Justin was watching happily from the snowmachine, holding a cup of hot chocolate in his mitten-covered hands. "Trapshootin' is new, though." And it worked. He loved the focus.

"Hey—" Declan jerked his chin toward the edge of the Retreat's forest. "The only animal that doesn't run away from gunfire." Logan finally saw what Declan was referring to. It was that bird—ptarmigan. "Some call them stupid chickens." Declan's amused gaze slid to Logan's. "Ready to hunt small game?"

Logan wished Lani could've been here for this. If he missed, which was likely, she'd get a good laugh. If he managed to kill the bird, maybe she'd be proud.

"I'm ready." He set down the shotgun and accepted Declan's long-range rifle.

"It's not anywhere near as good as Kyle's gear," Declan said, helping Logan adjust the scope. "The firing pin freezes sometimes."

It didn't freeze, but Logan did miss. He'd expected more of a recoil, so his body had been too tense. Luckily, ptarmigans weren't the sharpest tools in the shed; it didn't really move, and Logan killed it on the next try.

He grinned.

"Nice work." Declan clapped him on the back before trekking over to collect the dead bird.

"Can I try, Daddy?" Justin asked with a hopeful expression.

Logan chuckled and shook his head. "Not yet, baby. Ask me again when you start school." Jesus, did he really say that? Could he imagine helping Justin hold a gun at the age of seven?

After all the stories he'd heard from Patrick and Declan...yes. Yes, he could. He would do as many others who lived in Alaska and teach his son how to survive. Step by step. The first time Patrick and Declan's dad took them to a practice range, they were six. They hadn't been allowed to actually go out into the woods and hunt with their father until they were older, but...they'd started at six.

Justin was turning five this year. Logan had some time to prepare himself for hunting with his son. So he shook those thoughts for now and soon he got back to shooting clay pigeons in the air.

"Pull!"

Miss.

Logan had one week left here to work on his aim. After that, he didn't know where he'd practice, although it looked like Barrow was next. 'Cause fuck if Logan was gonna allow Kyle to mope around alone anymore.

"Pull!"

Hit.

*

"You sure there's nothing else we can do?" Joakim asked. The twenty-two-year-old was thrilled to be able to give his new wife their first home, but he was uncomfortable because he couldn't afford to buy it right away.

"I've told you, kid. It's fine." Kyle dumped the last of his shit outside. Roger would be here any minute to help him get it all to the airport. "The upkeep is yours and just pay whatever you can spare a month. The house ain't worth all that much—it'll be yours in no time." He closed the door behind himself and walked to the little living room. Some furniture remained; he didn't need it. Their personal stuff had been boxed up and was waiting outside. "Focus on your wife. And start preparing one of the rooms for the baby." It'd be either Kyle's old room or Lani's. Kyle's dad had slept in the living room by his precious TV.

Not having his dad around anymore was…fucked up. The old man was supposed to be there at the end of a day, grunting complaints about outsiders or the weather and gossiping like a woman about captains who weren't paying their crews enough.

"What do you mean?" Joakim looked at him strangely. "Tea's not pregnant."

Kyle's brows rose. When he'd taken Joakim and his twin brother hunting for a week in the Interior, Kyle had heard enough to know Tea was knocked up. Unless it was normal for young women to start craving things they'd never liked before, gag at smells they were used to, be down with the "flu" most mornings, and complain about various aches.

One week. One grumpy Joakim. And the odd comment a day about how guilty he felt for enjoying the solitude for a while *because*… Enter reason.

"If you say so," Kyle chuckled. "Just don't be too surprised if Tea's stomach *moves* one day."

Joakim was getting a little panicky. "Oh, shit. Oh shit, oh shit, oh shit—I gotta call her. She should still be at work."

Kyle laughed as he watched Joakim run out of the house. For privacy, Kyle assumed. Then when it was only him left, there was nothing to laugh about anymore. Instead, he got nervous as fuck because this was it. He was saying goodbye to the house he'd grown up in. Sure, it was staying in the family, but he wouldn't live here anymore.

Pinnuaq Bay was waiting and, hopefully, so were Logan and the cub.

Anyaa was right. It was time to move on, and his future wasn't in Barrow.

Bringing out his phone, he typed a quick message to Logan.

116

I'm sorry for everything. Can we talk when I get back from a fishing trip tomorrow morning? I miss you.

He pocketed his phone and gave the house a final glance, then went outside where Joakim was trying to get ahold of his wife. It didn't seem to be working, though Kyle didn't have time to care that much. Roger was here now, and after filling his truck—not for the first time today—Kyle wished Joakim well and said goodbye.

He called Lani on the way, knowing his surprise would make the girl smile again.

"*Suvat*, Uncle Kyle?" Lani mumbled in greeting.

"Nothing much. What's up with you?" Kyle made sure to keep a smile in his voice. "Spending time with your friends, or...?"

She snorted. "No, I'm cleaning my room."

Yeah, 'cause Kyle had requested it. Anyaa was in on the surprise, and Kyle wanted a clean room to raid in order for everything to be packed quickly.

"It won't be your room any longer," Kyle told her. "If you look in your grandma's room, you'll find boxes. Start packing, *miki*. I'll be there in five minutes."

That earned him a delighted gasp. "Am I finally moving home?"

He let her believe that for a bit. "Does that mean you can pack fast?" He dodged her question.

"The fastest!"

"Okay," Kyle chuckled. "I'll see you soon." Ending the call, he turned to a smirking Roger. "She's definitely stoked."

"Imagine how excited she'll be when you guys end up at the airport." Roger snickered.

Kyle was getting damn excited himself. Not only was he surprising Lani, but he was surprising Logan. And no one knew at the Retreat. He'd only spoken to Patrick a little and knew no one was leaving the grounds today.

Feeling his phone vibrating in his hand, Kyle checked it and saw Logan's reply.

Had you texted me an hour later, it would've been too late. I was getting ready to call Mitch to fly us to Barrow. Call me the second you get back from your trip, Shaw. Be safe.

Kyle could tell Logan was pissed. No "I miss you, too" or "sweetheart" said it all. Not that Kyle blamed him.

He'd do everything in his power to make it up to Logan, though. Starting in a few hours.

"Want me to wait outside?" Roger asked as they got to Anyaa's street.

"No, it's fine. Anyaa's driving us later," Kyle replied. He wanted to get his stuff shipped to Pinnuaq as soon as possible— which included all his personal belongings, a snowmachine, and three dogs. A friend would meet up with the pilot and take care of everything for Kyle until he got there. "Lani doesn't have that much at her grandmother's place, so we'll bring it later."

He checked his watch and saw it was almost noon.

Five hours from now, he'd see Logan.

CHAPTER 15

"Daddy, hurry!" Justin complained. "Gray wants out!"

"Easy, easy. I'm almost done." Logan tightened the towel around his hips and entered the bedroom across the narrow hallway in their cabin. It had been a long day out by the dock, and dinner would be served soon in the staff house. Logan was also bringing the blueprints for the work he'd do on the cabin in his spare time this summer.

On the outside, the eleven cabins looked the same, and Logan's was right next to Declan and Quinn's cabin. However, they didn't have a kid—hopefully, two—to consider, so Logan had drawn up plans to add a loft. He'd have to tear down the wall that separated the bedroom from the living room, only to restore it after making space for a second floor. The ceiling was already high with its vaulted design, so there'd be no need for exterior work. In the end, it would give them an extra bedroom that Justin and Lani could share until they got old enough to ditch the grownups and stay in the staff house.

In the past couple of weeks, that dream had seemed more and more distant, although the text he'd received from Kyle around lunchtime had given Logan hope. Maybe Kyle was ready to come out of his mourning or whatever he'd been busy doing while avoiding everyone around him.

To Logan's frustration, that included Lani. She had spoken to Kyle often enough, but he'd been away too much for her to live with him. Even if she had lots of support from other family members, Kyle was the one she needed the most.

"Uncle Quinn is outside with Kiery!" Justin hollered as Logan put on a fresh T-shirt. "Can I go out, too? I won't be alone!"

"What did I tell you?" Logan reminded somewhat patiently. "You wait until I'm ready." He stepped into a pair of boxer briefs followed by socks, sweats, and snow pants.

"But, Gray—!"

"That's enough, Justin." Logan emerged from the bedroom as he pulled on a hoodie. "It wasn't that long ago he was out. He can wait two minutes."

Justin had been over the moon when Logan told him to pick out a pup, and the excited kiddo had surprised everyone when he'd presented his choice. Rather than going with one of the newer pups, he'd picked one from Lola's litter, and they were over two years old by now.

"But he's brother to Kiery and Wuff!" Justin had responded. *"He even looks like Wuff!"*

It was true. Gray, as Justin had appropriately named the dog, had the same gray-white coat as Kyle's Wolf. The only trait that made them different was that one of Gray's ears wasn't pointing up.

"What's that?" Justin cocked his head, already bundled up in his snowsuit and boots.

"What's what?" Logan attached Gray's leash to his collar then walked over to the kitchen nook in the corner of the living room to grab the blueprints off the counter.

"Is that a plane, Daddy?"

That made Logan pause, and he tried to hear—there it was. "Sounds like it." He nodded. It was extremely early, though. Their work was all but done; Patrick, Logan, and Declan were gonna wrap up the last, and John and Alex would be the first ones to head home. *Tomorrow.* Not today.

Quinn and Declan were next to leave after that—the following week. Logan had no solid plans—not until Quinn's folks were shipping the few belongings Logan wanted here—so he'd stick around with Patrick and Sarah. Then in a week or so, the rest of the staff and Nina, Patrick's wife, were returning for the new season.

Once they were all ready, Logan and Justin stepped outside with Gray, and Logan turned to Quinn, who was standing with his hands in the pockets of his snow pants. Lucky bastard. Kiery was well-behaved and obeyed every command. Logan certainly had his work cut out if he wanted Gray to be as obedient. And he did.

"Is Patrick expecting a shipment or somethin'?" Logan asked.

"Not that I know of," Quinn answered. "Speaking of, are you sure you don't wanna go back with us to the city next week?"

"I'm sure." Logan had fallen for this place. The nature was amazing, and he enjoyed the rustic feel of the buildings and all the work they never ran out of. Of course it would get a little lonely in the beginning; Quinn and Declan weren't scheduled to return until June, and it was only March now. But Logan knew he'd be busy in no time. Besides, he refused to make plans for leaving until he'd spoken to Kyle.

Before he and Kyle knew what was gonna happen, Logan would distract himself with work, fishing, and practicing more with Declan's guns. The day Logan went back to Anchorage to sign off on Quinn's folks' shipment to him, he was gonna buy his own hunting gear, too.

"I honestly never saw this comin'." Quinn shook his head, smiling. "You've always liked a good hike, so I had hopes you'd wanna settle down in Anchorage. Up here? No way."

Logan let out a low laugh and looked over to where Justin was walking Gray. "I didn't see it comin', either." He had doubts sometimes, mostly concerning Justin and how he wouldn't always be able to play with kids his own age. But then Logan would remind himself of guests coming up here. Some had children with them, not to mention that Logan would bring Justin to Nome regularly.

"Were Mom and Dad pissed when you told them it was

official?" Quinn asked.

"Nah." They really hadn't been. "Pam was sad, but Hank said they now had two more reasons to come visit." He slid his gaze to Quinn and smirked. "Your dad wants you to take him fishin'."

"Of course he does." Quinn snorted. "He can keep dreamin'—or go with Declan. If flyin's scary here, wait 'til you get out on the sea. The waves are worse than hurricane season in Florida, I swear."

"Drama queen," Logan retorted.

"Daddy, look!"

Logan's head whipped around, and he saw Justin's wide eyes first. Then he saw where Justin was pointing—toward the airstrip.

Two people were walking this way. One tall, one very short. Logan's mind registered the mossy green camos Kyle wore often, and he definitely remembered the light purple, knitted beanie Lani had.

Fuck me twice.

"Dude," he heard Quinn say in awe.

Logan got his feet to move. Step by step, way too fucking slow—until his sluggish brain finally caught up. It would be a while before the shock settled, but at least he could fucking move.

"Hi!" Justin shouted, breathing heavily as he ran after Logan with Gray. "Hi, hi, hi! Hi, Lani! Hi, Kyle!"

Lani picked up her pace and started running, and Logan saw her blinding smile as he finally got nearer.

It was literally impossible to describe the joy that surged through Logan.

"Logan!" Lani laughed. Right before Logan reached her, she held out her arms then flew right into him. "Hi!"

"God, it's good to see you again, darlin'!" He spun her around, making her squeal, and hugged her tightly. "I can't believe you're actually here."

"Uncle Kyle wanted to surprise you," Lani giggled. "It's so good to be back!" She wriggled free to greet Justin, who'd reached them now, too. "Hey, Justin! Is this Gray?"

"Yeah! He's Wuff's brother!"

Logan left them to it, his eyes glued to Kyle. "You fucking

bastard." He grinned.

Kyle grinned back, closing the last distance. "What a greeting, *piv*." Fisting Logan's jacket, Kyle yanked him close and crashed their mouths together in a searing kiss.

Sweet goddamn reunion.

Logan cupped the back of Kyle's neck and pushed his tongue between Kyle's parted lips. They tasted each other for the first time in a month and gripped one another tightly.

"I've missed you." Logan spoke in a hushed tone in the middle of kisses that alternated between sweet and slow and deep and passionate. "Motherfucker—I was so pissed."

"I know." Kyle dipped down and buried his nose in the little crevice between Logan's jacket and jaw, seeking warmth. "I'm sorry. I was fucking miserable, Logan. If I'd heard your voice, I wouldn't have been able to finish everything up there. I was a shit—I'm sorry."

"You're here now." Logan's anger had already melted away. "Are you okay, though?" His fingers crept up underneath Kyle's beanie, and Logan gently scraped his nails along Kyle's scalp the way he liked it. "With your dad and everythin'..."

"I miss him, but I'm okay." Kyle shuddered and hummed in pleasure. "I'm ready to catch up on everything I missed." He lifted his head and gave Logan a deep, drawn-out kiss. "Lani gossiped during the flight. She told me you got a dog." He smiled, the kiss growing lazy. "She also told me about the cabin."

"I'm really happy here," Logan admitted. "I've sold my soul to Patrick." They both chuckled and pressed their foreheads together. "I'm his for four months of the year—at least. I hope it won't get in the way of whatever you and I end up doing."

"First of all," Kyle murmured, his gaze intense, "you're always mine—no matter where we are. But I suppose I can let Patrick use you for various construction projects." He smirked and placed a quick kiss to Logan's lips. "Second of all, is there room for me and Lani in that cabin of yours?"

Logan nodded, ready to be up front about every little thing. "I want it to be ours, Kyle. We can't exactly stay here all year-round, but when we do..."

"I love the sound of that." Happiness brightened Kyle's silvery gray eyes. "So if you bring one home to the table, it's only fair that I provide one, too."

Logan was prepared for this. Relationships came with sacrifices and compromises. He'd witnessed Quinn and Declan enough to see it working extremely well, and Logan was prepared to give Barrow a chance. If anything, Justin would be able to meet kids his age.

"So...Barrow's next?" Logan asked.

Kyle frowned as if confused. "Huh? Oh—no. No." He chuckled quietly. "I have a better place to show you. I love Barrow, and I'm looking forward to showing you and the garden gnome around the Arctic one day, but it's not home anymore."

Logan spluttered a short laugh, unable to help it. Kyle referring to Justin as a fucking gnome did it—every time. "All right," he snickered, "so if not Barrow, then where?"

"You'll see soon. My mom died when my brother and I were kids, and she left us a piece of land." Kyle smiled and glanced at something behind Logan. "It's above the peninsula. When you're ready to get out of here for a few weeks, we'll fly down there."

Logan could be ready after the weekend. Looking over his shoulder, he tried to see whatever Kyle was watching. Logan half expected to see Quinn and the others, but it was only Lani and Justin.

"I gotta say hey to the cub," Kyle murmured. "I missed the little shit. Do you think it's possible to hug him without getting any nasty surprises?"

Logan shook his head, amused beyond words. "What kind of surprise would that be?"

Kyle shrugged and inched closer to where the kids were petting Gray. "Fuck if I know. Maybe he'll break. Or sneeze in my face."

"You're too fuckin' adorable sometimes, sweetheart." Logan laughed. "Don't worry, he's pretty durable."

"I don't know." Kyle made a face. "I've discovered it's possible to love someone without liking him. No offense. I mean—fuck." He looked frustrated. "I like him too; he just scares the shit out of me."

There was some serious fluttering in Logan's chest. As a father, there was no bigger compliment than hearing the man he loved saying he liked—and loved, apparently—his son.

"He loves you too, you know," he said quietly. Seriously. "He missed you and Lani a lot."

"Yeah?" Kyle appeared uncharacteristically abashed. "Cool." He rubbed the back of his neck. "That bodes well for the future, I guess. I mean, we're gonna be like a family, so it's pretty good if we like each other."

That word—*family*—was the last straw for Logan. There was no way he could wait until they were alone. It had to be now. "Hey." He pulled Kyle close and kissed him. "I love you."

Kyle smiled widely and kissed him back harder. "Ditto, *piv*. I love you, too."

They must've looked ridiculous, both kissing each other's smiles. Logan couldn't wait for them to get some privacy so he could show Kyle just how much he loved him. Fuck, this was…indescribable.

"*Piv*," Logan repeated, grinning and shaking his head. "When can you tell me what it means? For all I know, you're calling me prick or somethin'."

Kyle let out a laugh and pressed a kiss to Logan's beard. "I've no issue telling you now. And, for the record, I don't know any Inupiat word for prick." Another kiss, this time to Logan's cold nose. "*Piv* is short for *piviuttaqqun* in Iñupiaq. It means love."

Logan wasn't even gonna try to pronounce it. Kyle made it seem effortless. It fucking wasn't.

"Love beats prick," he said with a crooked grin. "Don't expect me to learn, though." It seemed like a language you needed to be around from birth to figure out. "I'll leave the Inupiat talkin' to you and Lani. Or…Iñupiaq, whatever." He'd heard Kyle using both words.

"Inupiat is the people," Kyle answered. "It also describes the languages with one word, and Iñupiaq is the most common language in Barrow."

Logan let out a chuckle, knowing he looked confused. "Forget

I asked."

"That's nothing." Kyle smirked. "There're also countless dialects, and Lani's family happens to use several."

"Jesus," Logan muttered. "And I thought it was difficult to learn Spanish in school." He waved a hand at Justin and Lani. "Let's get greetings over with before my head explodes. Then we're rushin' through dinner."

"Why the rush, Ward?" As if Kyle didn't know.

"We have a bedroom in our new home to christen."

CHAPTER 16

"Want?" Justin stuck a spoonful of peas in Kyle's face.

"I have my own food," he told the tiny human.

Kyle couldn't fucking stop smiling. He felt like a tool, and he didn't care. For the first time, he wasn't merely returning to the Retreat as an employee or a friend. This was one of his homes now. With Logan, Lani, and the cub.

Logan, seated next to Kyle in the kitchen, shook his head. "You gotta finish all the vegetables, Justin. I've told you that."

Okay, so vegetables were important. Noted.

Kyle had a lot to learn.

"But I'm full," Justin replied, leaning back against Kyle's chest.

"So how long are you staying?" John asked.

"Well, we've spoken to Patrick." Logan nodded at Patrick, who nodded in return. "We'll work through this weekend and see if we can get on the same plane as Quinn and Declan next week."

"Shouldn't be a problem," Patrick said.

Quinn perked up. "Oh, does that mean you're coming with us to Anchorage?"

Logan lifted a brow at Kyle since he didn't know where they

CARA DEE

were going.

Kyle smiled. "No, we're going to my place near Katmai."

"Bear country, huh?" Declan grinned wryly. "We went there with our dad as kids." He jerked his chin at his twin brother.

"Really," Logan said flatly. "Just how may bears does it take for it to qualify as bear country?"

Kyle, Patrick, Declan, and John smirked and said, "Thousands."

"Great." Logan looked down at his food. "Sounds very safe."

"Have some faith in me, *piv*." Kyle leaned over and kissed Logan's shoulder. "Besides, you know how to protect us all now. Lani told me that you've been doing some trapshooting." And when he'd heard how good Logan was, Kyle had gotten a little hard, no lie.

"No wonder you wanted more dogs," Patrick chuckled.

With training, they'd be great for trapping and gathering; plus, Kyle would be hired on the spot for SAR missions if he provided dogs that were good trackers. But what Patrick implied was for the bears. The dogs would be their very own alarm system.

The good thing was that it got cold very quickly in that part of Alaska, so the bear season was short. Pinnuaq was surrounded by water, and the harsh winds drove bears up the mountains to hibernate.

"What will you be doing there for work?" Declan asked curiously.

"Hunting guide," Kyle responded with a nod. "We'll be right between two national parks, so the hunting grounds aren't big, but they're packed with wildlife."

"So you'll be teaching tourists how to hunt?" Sarah asked. She sighed. "Wonderful."

Kyle didn't dignify that with a response.

Cheeky Lani did. "I know, right?"

So did John. "Sarah, those *tourists* already know how to hunt and would be doing it elsewhere if Kyle weren't there. Katmai isn't for newbies."

Very true.

"Only puttin' this out there," Logan said, shifting in his seat to

128

face Kyle more fully, "you do know we're bringing a four-year-old, right?"

"Yes, dear." Kyle stifled his grin.

"Okay. Okay. Just wanna be clear. I trust you."

"I will be five fingers soon!" Justin held up his hand, right in Kyle's face.

"Good to know." Kyle nodded.

Everyone could probably tell Logan was skeptical about Pinnuaq. Kyle wasn't worried. He was, however, grateful that Logan didn't shoot him down before knowing every little detail. He was giving Kyle a chance—by default, trusting Kyle with Justin—and it mattered.

"So…" Alex took a swig from his beer. "This means you'll be flying with Valium boy next week."

Most of the guys cracked up, Kyle included.

"Y'all better stop teasin' me before I sic Declan on your asses," Quinn warned. "You'd punch 'em for me, wouldn't you, sweetheart?"

"Yes, dear," Declan deadpanned.

Logan chuckled. "I would've put his ass on YouTube."

"That does sound tempting," Declan mused.

"Justin, cover your ears," Quinn said before facing the rest. "Fuck you. Fuck all y'all."

"I heard that," Justin giggled.

"Da—um, Uncle Kyle, can we watch a movie later?" Lani asked.

Kyle nodded. "Sure." Glancing around him, he noticed how everyone had gone silent. Logan was smiling at his plate, Quinn—seated next to Lani—leaned over and kissed the top of her head. Lani herself was blushing scarlet.

What had Kyle missed?

"We have loads of leftover marshmallows and some other candy," Patrick said, squeezing Lani's hand. "Take it to your cabin. My wife's on a diet and would kill me if I have *temptations* lying around when she gets here." He looked up at the other guys. "She gained five pounds over Christmas, and suddenly she says she's an elephant. When I told her she was beautiful anyway, she almost had my head."

"I'm so glad I'm gay," Quinn said.

Declan smirked. "I'm glad you're gay, too."

"It's the 'anyway' that pissed her off," John told Patrick. "That single word let her know you were acknowledging the weight gain."

Kyle shook his head and placed an arm along the back of Logan's chair. "Wanna get out of here before they start bitching about periods and hair braiding?"

"Hell, yeah." Logan polished off the rest of his beer then stood up. "Thanks for dinner, John. It was great, but we're gonna head out. Let's go, kids."

"So friggin' domesticated." Quinn's green eyes flashed with mirth. "The only thing missin' is a minivan."

"Will you build the roads so we can use it?" Kyle stood up, too. The cub clung to him like a monkey, which was convenient. "It's good to be back. See you guys tomorrow."

It had already gotten late, so Kyle hoped it wouldn't take long before Lani and Justin fell asleep.

Once they were all bundled up and Lani and Justin had received a bag with way too much candy from Patrick, they left the staff house. They'd barely taken five steps before Logan stopped.

"Holy shit." He was looking up.

Following his gaze, Kyle saw that the lights were out, and both Wards were in awe. With the winter having been so harsh, the best they'd gotten so far was a green glow hidden behind clouds. Not tonight. Multicolored waves stretched across the crystal-clear night sky.

Lani started whistling softly, a lullaby Kyle's dad and brother had sung to her many times in the past.

"John whistled one night, too," Logan murmured. "Is there a reason?"

Kyle nodded, absently grabbing Lani's hand. "Some say it's bad luck. Others say it makes the lights dance for you."

"This is amazing." Logan picked up Justin since the snow was so deep, and he brought out his phone to snap off a photo of the sky. "Isn't it cool, baby?"

"Yeah." Justin's eyes were glued to the lights, too. "Look,

Daddy, they're movin'!"

Kyle smiled and tugged gently on Lani's hand so they could walk ahead. It had been a crazy day, and he wanted to make sure everything was all right. She'd excited to the point of tears when she learned they were coming here, not to mention they were moving down to Pinnuaq, but once the dust settled…who knew.

"You okay with all this, *miki*?" he asked quietly.

"Super okay." She grinned and hugged his arm. "I think Justin's gonna *love* Pinnuaq, and when we live up here, I don't have to go to school!"

Trust the ten-year-old to find joy in getting out of classes. "You'll have correspondence school," he reminded her.

"Yeah, yeah." She waved that off. "That's different. Logan's the best teacher."

Kyle wasn't even gonna pretend to be insulted. He sucked at helping her with homework.

"So you're on board with all of us living together and whatever?"

Lani giggled and looked up at him. "I think that's something you're supposed to ask me *before* we move, but *yes*. It's perfect."

"Brat," he chuckled and kissed the top of her head. He agreed, though. It was fucking perfect. "You'll be Justin's big sister." They reached the porch outside the cabin, and Kyle unzipped his jacket. "Don't get him in too much trouble." He winked at Lani.

She smirked, though it faded as they got indoors. She bit her lip, silent as she got rid of her jacket and snow pants.

"Something wrong?" he asked. Leaving the entryway, he glanced around the living room, smiling at the homey feel of it. Gray wagged his tail, leaving his makeshift bed in the corner between the window and the TV. Kyle noticed the fire needed to be stoked, so he crossed the room and opened the fireplace to throw some wood in.

Fuck, he loved this. Logan had told him briefly about the plans to add a loft for Lani and Justin, and until then, they'd share the pullout couch. And, as Lani had said, have movie nights all the time until they fell asleep.

"*Miki?*" He joined her by the entryway again and grabbed the bag of marshmallows and shit. "You didn't answer me."

Kyle made himself useful and brought the bag over to the kitchenette. In a cupboard, he found two bowls for marshmallows and fuckin' gummy bears, and in another he found two mugs so he could make hot chocolate for the underage sprites.

Kyle missed milk. None of this powdered hot cocoa shit, and not the milk in Barrow that bankrupted anyone. He missed the jugs he could buy for a few bucks in Anchorage. They'd have to go there soon to buy supplies, anyway.

"Can I ask you something, Uncle Kyle?"

"Of course." He placed two mugs of water in the microwave. Would he ever take electricity for granted? Probably not. He was so used to battery packs that died way too quickly, fireplaces in every room, outhouses, water that had to be delivered, and generators that always broke.

"If Justin will be my brother..." Lani joined him and fiddled with the edge of a candy bowl. "Does that mean you and Logan will be my parents?"

"Oh." Kyle hadn't thought of it that way, and it kinda petrified him. He felt his hands beginning to sweat at the mere thought of being a parent. At the same time, he already was the legal guardian of his niece. "I, uh..." Shit, was it hot in here? He would *fail*. Miserably. He'd fuck those two kids up. Right up there. "I mean—" He cleared his throat. "I suppose so, in a way. But don't worry." He tried to make light of it. "I'll always be your Uncle Kyle, and you can call Anyaa every time I do anything stupid. All right?"

Lani smiled, though it looked a little forced. "Yeah. That's good. Thanks." With her head down, she took the two bowls to the coffee table.

Kyle's forehead creased. See? He was already screwing up. He'd clearly said something wrong now.

Before he could fuck shit up further, Logan and Justin entered the cabin with matching grins.

Logan seemed to notice the awkward tension though, and he frowned as he squatted down to help Justin with his snowsuit.

"What's wrong?" he mouthed.

Kyle shrugged helplessly and rubbed the back of his neck, 'cause fuck if he knew.

Logan glanced between Lani and Kyle again then murmured, "I'll take care of it." He smiled down at Justin. "Hey, can you show Kyle where the pillows and the blankets are in the bedroom?"

Justin nodded and ran past Kyle, who followed after taking out the mugs from the microwave.

It didn't take more than approximately seventeen seconds to get blankets and pillows for Justin and Lani, but Kyle figured it would take longer for Logan to fix whatever he'd done wrong earlier.

Leaving him alone with another kid probably wasn't a good idea, though.

Kyle had a feeling Logan would spend the rest of their lives putting out proverbial fires.

"So, how are you?" Kyle sat down on the edge of the bed.

Justin stared at him.

Great. "Do you like that we're gonna live here half the year now?" Kyle went on.

The gnome nodded. "Yes. Daddy says we're gonna live here when there's lots of snow."

"That's right. The summer, too. Winter and summer."

"The snow's the best." Justin grinned.

Well, this was going nowhere fast.

"We're flying to our other home next week." Kyle was running out of crap to say. How long would Logan need? "In the spring, we'll see bears every day. We'll go egg-picking at the cliffs and shit. And in the summer, we'll be back in time to follow the bears upriver to find a fuckload of salmon."

"Okay," Justin giggled. "What's a sammon?"

"A type of fish," Kyle told him. "You've had it."

"Okay."

Kill me now, Kyle thought with a groan. He fell back against the bed and stared up at the ceiling. How did Logan do this? He was an amazing father to Justin. And Lani, Kyle had to admit. Because that was exactly what Logan had become. Effortlessly, it seemed.

"Hi!" The tiny human jumped up on the bed too, and caused Kyle to let out an *oomph* when Justin nearly crushed his balls. "Are you sleepy?"

"I'm getting there." Kyle situated Justin higher up, his little legs on either side of Kyle's middle. "How can something so cute and small be so goddamn scary?" He reached up and brushed away a lock of hair from Justin's forehead. "You need a haircut. That's my rule of thumb—once the hair gets in my eyes and obstructs my view when I'm trying to aim, I let Lani's grandmother take out the kitchen shears."

"Daddy says I'm too big to suck my thumb now," Justin replied.

Right. "Listen to him. He knows what he's doing. I don't."

"I think you're doin' a great job," Kyle heard Logan murmur from the doorway. Tilting his head, Kyle saw Logan approaching with a soft smile. "Justin, Lani's waiting with hot chocolate and a movie in the livin' room."

"Okay." Justin grinned and climbed off Kyle and the bed.

Kyle sat up. "Anything I can do?"

"Nah." Logan leaned down and kissed him chastely. "I'll go make their bed and lock up—you go take a shower or somethin'."

A lazy smirk tugged at Kyle's mouth. "Are you saying I stink?"

"No, but I was thinkin' I'd join you."

A shower *did* sound awfully good right about now.

CHAPTER 17

Kyle stood under the hot spray, just about to reach for the bodywash, when Logan entered the bathroom. A quiet snick let Kyle know the door was locked, and he saw Logan undressing through the half-transparent shower curtain.

"Any room for me?"

"Always." Kyle pushed the curtain aside and let Logan step into the tub. "Fuck." His mouth watered at the sight of Logan's naked body.

"That's what I'm hoping for." Logan grinned, and the bastard had even brought lube. "Can you be quiet?"

"Can you?" Kyle shot back softly.

"We'll try." Logan chuckled huskily and reached around Kyle to set the lube on the little shelf and take the bodywash. "Turn around. I wanna get my hands on you."

Kyle was more than happy to oblige, so he turned his back to Logan and rolled his shoulders. After spending the past two days packing, he couldn't help but groan under his breath when Logan began soaping him up with firm hands.

"Shit, that feels good." Kyle's chin dropped to his chest. With the water pouring down, the suds disappeared almost immediately.

It didn't matter. Logan's hands traveled smoothly over his back, rubbing out kinks and raising goose bumps.

"I missed you." Logan dropped an openmouthed kiss to Kyle's shoulder, his skilled hands sliding to Kyle's front. At the same time, the last distance was closed between them, and Kyle shuddered at the feel of Logan's hard cock against his ass.

"I missed you, too." Kyle tilted his head back next so he could kiss Logan's jaw. "*Jesus.*" Fingers wrapped around Kyle's erection and stroked him slowly. "I wanna fuck you."

"God, yes," Logan mumbled against the skin on Kyle's neck. "It's been way too long."

"Yeah?" Kyle's possessive side took over, and he turned around. "You've missed my cock?"

"More than I missed the rest of you." Logan grinned at his joke. "How do you want me?"

"Hands on the wall behind you."

Logan complied while Kyle grabbed the lube. Christ, his fingers were trembling. Pouring a generous amount of the slippery liquid in his hand, he slid it between Logan's ass cheeks. To relax him, Kyle used his free hand to stroke Logan's cock and kissed his muscled back.

"You know what I love?" Kyle murmured. "That I'll be the only one to own this sweet ass." His middle finger circled Logan's tight hole and slowly pushed inside. "It's all mine, baby."

"Yeah—fuck. Yeah." Logan panted and pushed back. A quiet groan slipped through his lips as Kyle fucked him slowly with two, then three fingers.

With a careful twist, Kyle pressed down on Logan's prostate and massaged it gently. It made Logan tilt his head to bite down on his bicep. His knees buckled slightly, too.

"Mine to finger-fuck," Kyle went on quietly, staring at his fingers disappearing into Logan. "Mine to lick, mine to drill my cock into and fill with my come."

"Jesus fuckin' Christ, Kyle," Logan breathed out. "I want it. Now—right now."

Kyle didn't rush it. He spent another few minutes fingering Logan's ass and stroking his cock at the same time—until a clear string of pre-come dripped down the tip. Only then did Kyle draw back and apply lube to his cock. Next, he nudged Logan's feet farther apart and stepped closer.

He teased Logan, rubbing the head of his erection against Logan's slick opening. Kyle clenched his jaw to stay quiet, and then he pushed forward a couple inches.

Logan hissed a curse, the sound muffled by the flesh of his arm.

"Push back," Kyle whispered in a gravelly voice. "Take my cock, *piv.*" He eased in slowly, always overwhelmed by the tightness. "Fuck, you feel good." He paused, buried all the way in, and nuzzled Logan's neck.

The bathroom was soon filled with shallow breaths, quiet moans, and whispered curses.

In and out in quick thrusts, Kyle filled Logan's ass over and over.

"Don't touch your dick." Kyle gripped Logan's hips at bit harder and rammed into him. "That come is mine." He bit down on Logan's shoulder to muffle his sounds. When he straightened his legs to stand an inch taller, he managed to rub over Logan's prostate with each pass.

At least, Logan's quickened breathing and moaning said so. "Oh God, more, more, more…"

Kyle clenched his jaw and went faster, his orgasm coming way too rapidly for his liking. But he guessed it wasn't weird after having been away from Logan for so long.

Only a few minutes later, Kyle's climax rushed through him. With a strangled growl, he shoved his cock deep inside Logan's ass and felt pulses of come soaking the tight muscle he was buried in.

He couldn't fucking breathe.

The steam from the hot water fogged the air.

"*Kyle.*" The pleading note in Logan's voice brought Kyle back.

He groaned quietly and shivered, slowly pulling out his spent cock. *Goddamn gorgeous.* The sight made Kyle swallow hard, another round of lust flaring up. He stared at Logan's used ass, rivulets of water mixing with lube and Kyle's release that seeped out.

"Turn around and put one foot up on the edge of the tub,"

Kyle instructed quietly. Shit, he was still trying to catch his breath. Which wasn't made easier by kneeling down and being so close to Logan's throbbing cock. Not saying a word, he slowly slid two fingers between Logan's thighs and up to stroke his fucked ass. Then he fisted Logan's cock with his free hand and took him in his mouth.

Logan hissed and cupped the back of Kyle's head.

Kyle sucked Logan's cock hard and greedily, at the same time as he fingered him and massaged his prostate. Kyle enjoyed bottoming as much as topping, though his prostate wasn't as sensitive as Logan had discovered his was. Every time Logan's thighs shook and the faintest whimpers slipped through his lips, Kyle wanted to slam him up against a wall and fuck him all over again. It was the hottest thing he'd ever experienced.

"You close, baby?" Kyle closed his lips over the head of Logan's cock and teased his tongue across the slit.

Logan nodded quickly, his teeth firmly embedded in his lower lip.

Not wanting to deny him any longer, Kyle gripped the base tightly, sucked as much as he could into his mouth, and rubbed persistent little circles over that spot in Logan's ass. Pre-come coated Kyle's tongue, and he moaned at the salty flavor.

"Yeah—fuck," Logan panted, and he began fucking Kyle's mouth in quick, shallow thrusts. "So close. Oh my God."

When Kyle hummed around the length, Logan let out a choked noise and pushed forward on pure instinct. *Fuck, yes.* Kyle breathed deeply through his nose and swallowed the first stream of come. Then the next and the next.

For Christ's sake, Kyle was already getting hard again.

Logan fell back against the wall and groaned tiredly. "I can barely stand."

Kyle smiled to himself and kissed his way up Logan's body. "So let's continue this in the bedroom."

"Yeah." Logan leaned in and kissed Kyle deeply, tasting himself. "You might wanna talk to Lani first, though." He hummed, and Kyle tried to remember why he needed to speak to Lani. Logan's kisses were too fucking drugging. "I'll wait under the covers for you."

The memory came back puzzle piece by puzzle piece, and Kyle felt stupid. And then nervous. "How did I fuck up before, and what did I fuck up?"

"You didn't fuck up, sweetheart." Logan chuckled quietly and turned off the water. "You just told her what you thought she wanted to hear when she wanted the opposite." He smiled at Kyle and then reached for a towel. "You've basically been her father for the past five years, Shaw. Us moving in together and becomin' a family is makin' her want the labels, too."

Kyle frowned and wrapped a towel around his hips. "Wait, so you're saying she wants to..." *call me Dad?*

His stomach did a somersault at that. Stepping out of the tub, he stared down at his feet, processing. A part of him wanted to run out to the living room and say of-fucking-course she could call him Dad, but Jesus, the title made it so official. It was easier to be a clueless uncle than a bad father.

"She asked me, too," Logan murmured. Kyle's gaze snapped up. "I made sure she knew I'd be honored to be her dad, but she has to talk to you first."

"Oh," Kyle mouthed. Furrowing his brow, he averted his eyes again and toweled off quickly. His heart was racing. It was...goddamn overwhelming. It was as if his chest had to be physically expanded to make room for all these fucking emotions. "How can you know all these things?" he whispered, still not looking up. He was raw inside. "I don't know shit about—"

"Let me stop you right there," Logan said mildly. "You gotta quit thinkin' that way. Look at the facts instead. For the past five years, you and your dad have taken care of Lani, and would you change a single thing about her? She's a happy girl, she gets good grades, her elders are proud of her, and you're her hero just for existing and being there for her."

Kyle released a shaky breath and scrubbed his hands down his face.

"Hey." Logan stepped close and nudged up Kyle's chin. "I know what you're feelin', okay? I was there two years ago. I'm still lost sometimes. Then Quinn's mom sorta made me realize that kids love us even when we screw up. And we *will* screw up, Kyle. But we'll always be there for them, too."

Kyle looked away again, though he nodded. He did agree with that. Being there for Lani—and the cub—was a given. And when Kyle thought about it, he admitted that he considered Lani his. As in, more than a niece. He hadn't put a daughter label on it, yet that was the only thing missing, wasn't it? She belonged to him in every other aspect. She was his, and had been for years.

"All right." He sighed and nodded again. "I'll talk to her. And you better teach me how to pick up on these things."

"I'll do my best." Logan smirked and opened the cabinet to take out his toothbrush. "But would you be okay if she called me Dad, too?"

"Of course." Kyle frowned. To him, that was obvious. "She idolizes you, Logan." Then he thought about Justin. "How do we bring this up with the gnome? I don't do well with awkward situations, and I wouldn't know how to explain this crap to him."

Logan's smirk softened in the mirror, and he turned to face Kyle fully. "First of all, do you *want* Justin to call you Dad?"

"It makes sense," Kyle said. "Plus, I want to have a claim when I pick him up from school and shit. Strangers gotta know he's mine, too."

"I love you." Logan was both grinning and shaking his head. Kyle was pretty sure Logan's eyes looked glassy, too. "You may not see it, but you show me how much you care for him and Lani all the time—in your own way."

"Okay… Um, I love you, too." However, this didn't help Kyle with what to say when he left the bathroom. "So what do I tell him?"

Logan snorted a chuckle and turned to the mirror again. "I wouldn't worry about it. He's gonna hear you when you talk to Lani, and he'll come to his own conclusion. If he has questions, he'll ask. He ain't exactly shy."

That didn't erase Kyle's fears much, but he decided to wing it. He wouldn't be able to prepare himself enough for a thing like this, so here went nothin'.

"Wish me luck." Kyle steeled himself and left the bathroom,

stalking straight into the living room where two tiny humans were bundled up under the covers on the pullout couch watching some Disney movie.

He came to a stop and felt stupid. Having just been in the humid bathroom, there was a nip in the air that made him wanna cover up, but fuck it. He tightened the towel around his hips and sat down on the edge by Lani's feet.

She glanced away from the movie and looked Kyle in the eye apprehensively.

"Did you take a bath?" Justin asked around a mouthful of gummy bears.

"A shower, yeah." Kyle cleared his throat, nervous as fuck. "Logan told me what you talked about, *miki*," he murmured. "I didn't know you wanted…that. If I'd known, you know, I, uh, I would've said yes. Right away." Okay, the words were out there. That counted for something. "I mean it." He laid a hand on Lani's foot and squeezed it gently. "You, Justin, and Logan are everything for me, and you've already been mine since you were two shits high."

Lani smiled shyly but didn't say anything.

Kyle puffed out his cheeks and then blew out a breath. "What I'm saying is…if you wanna call me Dad instead of Uncle, I'm extremely fine with that. Same goes for Logan—he cried like a little girl, he was so happy." Okay, that wasn't even remotely true, though it made Lani and Justin giggle. And since he was on a roll, he thought, *fuck it*, and addressed Justin next. "You're included in all this as well, cub. If you ever wanna call me Dad or whatever—like Lani might with Logan—that's cool."

Justin sat up straighter and cocked his head. "You can have two daddies?"

Well, shit. Kyle didn't wanna go into a discussion on gender equality and families that had two moms or two dads, so he hoped a simple yes would suffice.

"Yeah. Definitely." He nodded. "I mean, I'm not really a *daddy* type. That's Logan. And—between you and me—something Uncle Quinn might call Uncle Declan in the sack, but that's just a theory. Anyway…yeah, feel free to call me Dad. If you want."

Lani scrunched her nose. "What kind of sack?"

"The kind you'll learn about when you're in your thirties," Kyle replied. "So don't tell Logan I mentioned it."

"Too late."

Shit. Kyle glanced over to the hallway between the bathroom and bedroom and saw Logan standing there, looking like he was about to explode with laughter.

Laugh it up, fucker.

"Okay, my job is done here," Kyle decided. He clapped his thighs and then stood up. Being closest to Lani, he leaned over and kissed her on the forehead. "Love you, *miki.* You have a milk 'stache from the cocoa." Next, he rounded the pullout and kissed the top of Justin's head. "Love you too, gnome. Even if you look like a hamster when you have your cheeks full of candy."

He laughed madly. "What'sa gnome?"

"*You.*" Kyle smirked and started to leave. "Have fun brushing his sugary teeth later," he told a grinning Logan before he ducked into their bedroom.

Closing the door behind himself, he leaned back against it and felt his heart hammering in his chest.

Jesus Christ, his life had changed.

He had a fucking family. Some way, somehow, he'd ended up with two kids. Two of them. Two *kids.*

And why the hell did that excite him?

Well, the sense of terror was still there, but perhaps that came with parenting.

He hoped so.

EPILOGUE

Three years later...

Logan leaned casually against the corner of the simple school building, waiting for Lani to come out. With a total of only sixty-something students, there was hardly a need for a bigger building. In Lani's class alone, there were nine kids. In Justin's, there were thirteen.

From this corner, he could see the entire town center of Pinnuaq Bay, which consisted of dirt roads lined up with a few Inuit souvenir shops, the town's only motel and pub, a grocery store, the small church, the post office, a dealership for ATVs and snowmachines, and one store with overpriced fishing and hunting gear. Surrounding the center was everything from shacks and sheds to two-story apartment buildings and nicer cabins.

It was home for Logan and the two hundred other residents. Well, Logan didn't actually live *in* town. He lived in the middle of the bay, and it had been love at first sight.

Checking his watch, he wondered why Lani was taking so long. Maybe she was getting some extra assignments, he reasoned with himself. School didn't let out for the summer until next week, but they were heading up to the Retreat first thing tomorrow morning to spend the next three months there.

"Dad?"

Logan pushed off the wall and looked toward the entrance, spotting Lani running down the steps.

"You're home!" She smiled widely and hurried over to him.

"Got back a few hours ago." He hugged her tightly and kissed the top of her head. "Hold on." He was pretty sure he'd seen something different with her, so he broke the hug and cupped her cheeks. *What the fuck.* "I was only gone for four days—you didn't wear makeup before." It wasn't much, but he wasn't exactly fond of the glossy shit on her lips. They were fucking *pouty*, and he knew very well what boys thought about all hours of the day.

"Meh, at least you're not shouting at me." Lani shrugged and smiled sweetly, flipping her silky black hair over her shoulder.

"Yeah, I can imagine Kyle wasn't happy to see that," Logan grumbled. "Come on, let's go home. I parked over there."

They walked together to the small parking lot off the school grounds, and Logan stuck the key into the ATV.

"How was the trip?" she asked, getting on behind him.

"Rainy. Good catch." Logan could hold his own when it came to hunting, though once they moved here, they noticed he had a better knack for fishing.

Since Pinnuaq Bay wasn't the place for construction, he'd learned and adapted quickly, and now he did a little bit of everything. He'd found a daredevil inside himself who enjoyed taking fellow adventurers fishing along the dangerous cliffs. With Kyle as his teacher, Logan had also become skilled enough to take smaller groups of hikers for some off-trail camping and wildlife viewing in Katmai National Park.

The engine rumbled to life, putting a stop to the conversation for now, and Logan drove out of the town. Soon, they were surrounded by forest, with the exception of a cabin here and there.

A narrow path took them down toward the water, and the trees gave way to a pebbled beach and an extraordinary view of their home. In the middle of the bay, there was a small island.

Rounded, elevated some five feet above sea level, and roughly the size of a hockey rink.

Two cabins faced the beach and protected them from most of the winds coming in from the ocean, and what they didn't do, the three dozen trees did.

Logan loved to call it home as much as he loved to wake up every morning to the sun rising over the forest-covered mountains behind them right now.

Lying next to the man he planned to spend the rest of his life with only made it better.

Coming to a stop, Logan let the ATV idle as he walked over to their shed on the beach. With the number of bears and other animals that roamed the area, they couldn't leave anything out. They even had to repair the shed almost every year.

Logan opened the door and returned to the vehicle. Lani had dismounted it and gone over to the small dock.

"Are Dad and Justin home?" she called.

"Not yet." He carefully drove the ATV into the shed where two snowmachines and two inflatable rafts were housed. Then he locked up and joined Lani at the dock. "I'm tryin' not to think about it."

For the past couple of months, Kyle had gone out into the woods with Justin two or three times a week. They left around dawn and came home before dinner. *With* dinner. Justin was Kyle's shadow, learning and observing. Their son was so obsessed with it that he'd managed to convince Kyle to let him be sick from school today. Since it was the last day and all...

"So where's the second boat?" Lani asked, getting into the one Logan always used.

"They probably took it with them." Logan lowered the engine into the water. "Justin wanted to see more upriver, and Kyle loves to indulge him."

Understatement, really. Lani had never lost her interest in hunting and trapping; however, it was different with her. She wanted to know everything, she just didn't particularly feel the need to live, breathe, and shit nature. Justin, on the other hand, seemed to have developed the same love for the wilderness Kyle had.

Logan didn't mind at all, although he preferred to leave it to Kyle because he couldn't do it himself. He was too overprotective, which would only hold Justin back. Even Logan knew that.

Sitting down, Logan started the engine and maneuvered them away from the dock. The island was only some fifty yards out, so it wasn't a long ride. But it definitely provided them with the protection they needed. Bears could obviously swim, and they had four dogs on the grounds to let Logan and the others know when a stray bear ventured out there. It only happened a couple times a year maybe, and Kyle called it takeout delivery.

When the bears came out of hibernation in the spring, they could sometimes see up to ten bears walking along the beach and digging for mussels.

Logan smirked to himself, remembering the first time he'd woken up to see a handful of bears moseying along the shore. He'd freaked out and wondered how the fuck the kids were gonna get to school now, and Kyle and Lani had only laughed.

"Ward, here in Alaska, you don't tell your teacher the dog ate your paper. You say there's a moose in the yard and you get a pass. Or in our case, bears."

"What'cha grinning at?" Lani asked.

"Bear country," Logan summed it up. "It really took me a while to understand what living *with* the wildlife entailed, didn't it?"

Lani giggled. "Well, it could've been worse. Remember when Nana and Pop visited?" She raised a brow.

Oh yeah, that had been...something else. A couple years ago, Quinn's parents had come up to Alaska. They spent a week in Anchorage with Quinn and Declan, and then they all came out to Pinnuaq. At the same time, Lani's Grandma Anyaa was visiting, too.

Talk about cultures colliding. Pam had fallen fast for Lani and insisted on being Nana for her too, and it had only led to Pam being more terrified of all the dangers here. She was constantly fussing, whereas Anyaa was tsk'ing and practically ushering Lani out into the wild.

Hank loved it here. Pam definitely preferred Anchorage.

"Hey, Dad, can I ask you a question *without* you going

bananas?"

That didn't sound good to Logan. "Last year when you said that, you wanted to go on a date with that James boy from your school." To which Logan had laughed and said *hell, no.* She was lucky he hadn't told Kyle about that. For fuck's sake, she had only turned fourteen two weeks ago.

"That was so long ago!" Lani argued. By then, they reached the dock on the island, so Logan killed the engine and secured the boat. "This is totally different."

"Is it about boys?"

"Well..."

"The answer is no." He got out of the boat and held out a hand for her.

She didn't take it. "You don't even know what I want!"

"Probably somethin' you're too young for," he muttered and followed her up the dock. Then he called after her. "It doesn't matter anyway, Ilannaq! We're out of here at six tomorrow morning!"

Lani whirled around and glared at him, standing some twenty feet away. "*That* should worry you."

"What's that supposed to mean?" Logan gave her a hard stare.

"Do you wanna hear me out or not?" she challenged.

Jesus. Being a parent of a teenager was not fucking easy. How did you protect your children from growing up too fast when it seemed that was all they wanted?

"Fine." Logan folded his arms over his chest and waited. "Let's hear it."

Their staring contest wasn't over yet, though. Lani tended to turn to Logan first with her problems because—believe it or not—he was a lot mellower than Kyle. Right now he guessed she was wondering if it was worth it.

"Okay, there's this boy," she said. "Nothing has happened, and I don't even know if he likes me."

"He probably does," Logan replied dryly. He didn't like thinking about it, but his daughter was growing up to be the kind of girl every fucking boy her age gawked at. He was thankful she remained fairly oblivious to it, though. Looks didn't seem to be

147

important to her.

"He sent me a text." Lani flushed. "I was curious... I mean— I'm not sure what it means..."

Something cracked Logan's armor, and he tried to calm down a bit. Lani was obviously struggling, and he wanted to help her.

"What does it say?" he asked, gentler now, and approached her.

She bit her lip. "I, um, I can show you, I guess." She dug a hand into the pocket of her pink windbreaker and retrieved her phone.

Logan stepped closer to peer down at the screen and then cocked a brow at whomever she had named "Cutie" with a bunch of emoticon hearts in her phone.

The latest message read, ***It's gonna be good seeing u soon. I've missed u.***

Logan honestly felt sad. Wasn't she too young for this? Had it already begun? Motherfuckers trying to steal her from Logan and Kyle?

"Does he m-mean like a friend or-or more?" Lani stammered.

"Oh, most likely more," Logan said reluctantly. "Who's it from, darlin'?"

Lani hesitated for a beat before mumbling, "Jax."

It was official. Logan wanted to strangle someone. A sixteen-year-old boy in this case. Holy fuck, Logan was *pissed*.

"He's..." He couldn't even speak, he was so angry. "You—" Goddamn. He pinched the bridge of his nose and screwed his eyes shut. "*Jax?*"

Suddenly, he didn't wanna go to the Retreat at all.

"He's changed, Dad," Lani whispered.

"Ha!" Logan barked out a humorless laugh and stalked away from her. "That's rich." He passed their four dogs that were chained to four doghouses outside the cabin Logan and Kyle lived in. Lani and Justin had their own rooms on the second floor, though they preferred the attic in the second cabin. It was mostly storage for gear and an office for their wildlife business, then with the second floor as a game room. For Lani, it was also a place where she could use Logan and Kyle's computer to go online and talk to her friends, which was a privilege Logan certainly reconsidered now.

He unlocked the door and stomped inside his house, shrugging out of his windbreaker and flannel shirt, leaving him in baggy cargos and a T-shirt. Beer—he needed a fucking beer.

Maybe Kyle would take up drinking once this got out. Seriously, *Jax*. Of all fucking people in the world.

Lani stood in the doorway as Logan took a swig.

"Need I remind you that he nearly burned down the staff house last year?" he asked impatiently.

"You're exaggerating! They put it out, and it was only, like, *one* wall in Jax's room," Lani said. "Patrick and Nina forgave him."

Logan scoffed. "Of course they did. They're his parents now." Kind of. They'd taken in Jax and his little brother Caleb two years ago. To say Jax was trouble was putting it mildly, but Patrick and Nina seemed to have endless patience for it.

Caleb was a sweetheart. At the age of eight, he also got along great with Justin, who was seven now. They were attached at the hip when they were together. But Jax? Nah, motherfucker.

"You're gonna tell Dad, aren't you?" Lani's bottom lip trembled.

Logan looked away from that and nodded. "Damn right, I will."

He wasn't unreasonable; he knew Jax had been through way too much. His mother had bailed when Caleb was only one, leaving him and Jax with an alcoholic and abusive father. It had eventually gotten out, and Jax and Caleb had gone from foster home to foster home in their home state—Arizona. Jax had always fucked it up somehow, usually with some crime. He'd stolen cars, vandalized schools, been in countless fights, and had already spent time in juvie.

Patrick and Nina were his last hope. In two years, Jax would be eighteen, and the next crime could be paid for behind real bars.

Logan had limits. Lani was that limit.

"You're not being fair," Lani choked out. "You don't understand him. He's done stupid things because-because he didn't wanna get close to anyone. His mom and dad hurt him so much,

Dad. He didn't wanna be hurt again, so…"

"So he did the hurting instead?" Logan didn't like how mature Lani sounded. The voice was still that of a young girl, but she was wise. She was growing up. "I'm sorry, it's not good enough for me, darlin'." He narrowed his eyes at her. "How much have you been talkin' to him?"

Lani shrugged. "Lots. We talk on the phone almost every day."

"Hmph."

"He likes to talk to me." The girl with an obvious crush appeared. "I help him with homework and stuff. He's behind, and he is comfortable with me."

Logan sighed heavily. Some of his anger had dissipated, but *fuck.* "I gotta talk to Kyle about this."

God, he needed Kyle here. Right fucking now.

*

In the late afternoon the following day, Logan watched the Retreat come into view as Mitch's son brought the plane down.

Besides the roaring of the engines and Justin humming happily to some song, the silence between Logan, Kyle, and Lani was deafening.

To say that Kyle had been furious when Logan told him was the understatement of the year. Even three years into their relationship, Kyle was quick to berate himself and say he was clueless about parenting. Even so, he'd been damn quick to throw out every clichéd parent threat in the book.

"You're grounded 'til you're forty, Ilannaq!"

"Remember that ATV you've been eyeing? Forget about it!"

"Can you tell me what Logan and I have done to deserve this? Huh? Do you want to put us underground already?"

"You can kiss your phone goodbye!"

Lani still had her phone, but Logan wasn't sure Kyle had been kidding about grounding her until she was forty.

"Oh, that was a big one!" Justin cracked up as the plane bounced along the runway. "Uncle Quinn's here already, right?"

Logan nodded. "They got here with supplies about an hour ago."

They were at full capacity this season, which meant a lot of work and good money, and Logan's first task was to go hunting with Kyle. He didn't know if that was still a go. He had a feeling Kyle would want one of them to constantly keep an eye on their girl.

Logan was torn about it. His opinion hadn't exactly changed, except he couldn't help but think back on how his own parents had treated him. He'd basically been pushed aside because he didn't go for the career they wanted, and it was Quinn's parents who'd been there. Through good times and bad.

As the plane came to a stop, Kyle was the first one out the door, and Logan removed the harnesses from the dogs in the back so they could jump out, too.

In the distance, Logan saw a group of guests returning from a hike—presumably in the Preserve—and Nina was leading them.

Logan helped Justin and Lani out of the plane as Kyle unloaded all their luggage.

"Welcome back, guys!" Nina waved from some twenty yards away.

"No red carpet, hon?" Logan hollered.

She laughed and continued on with the tourists.

It was T-shirt weather for Alaskans. For former Floridians, a hoodie was better. Logan wore one, and Quinn—who was approaching from the Retreat with Declan—wore one, too.

"Dad?" Lani asked Kyle carefully. "Is it still okay that I sleep in the staff house?"

Kyle laughed. "That's funny, *miki*. Yeah, *sure*—you go right ahead. Sleep right next door to Jax." The laughter died. "No."

Lani slumped her shoulders and started carrying two bags toward their home.

"How's it goin', sweetie?" Quinn smiled widely at Lani, who merely passed him with a huff. Quinn raised a wobbly brow at Logan. "Did'ju fight and drama or somethin'?"

That sentence...didn't work at all. Logan turned to Declan. "I'm assuming the Valium hasn't worn off yet."

Justin, however, was happy to jump into Quinn's arms for a hug.

"You assume correctly." Declan nodded with a dip of his chin. "You look happy to be back, kiddo." He ruffled Justin's hair.

"Yeah. Dad's promised me we can go fishin' tomorrow." Justin poked Quinn's nose. "Wanna come with?"

Logan pointed to Kyle, the dad in question.

"Patrick and Caleb are coming, too," Kyle said.

"Nah, me and stormy seas don't go well together," Quinn chuckled. "So, what's thish—*thisss*...drama with Lani? My tongue feels weird."

"You're funny," Justin giggled.

"Lani's crushin' on Jax," Logan grumbled.

"Oh!" Quinn laughed. "I bet y'all are just *thrilled*. In Jax's defense, though...he's calmed down a lot."

Yeah, yeah.

*

Once the dogs were in the new yard between their and Quinn and Declan's cabin and all their luggage unpacked, Kyle fell back against the mattress in the bedroom, and Logan wasn't far behind.

"I don't like this." Kyle drew Logan close and buried his face in the crook of Logan's neck. He smelled so fucking good, a mixture of aftershave and mosquito repellent. "I won't budge."

Logan hummed, which bugged Kyle because he wasn't sure what Logan was thinking. Kyle needed them both to be very against this crap between Lani and Jax.

"Hey—" Kyle nudged his nose against Logan's chin and kissed him there. "I love you. Don't leave me alone in this fight."

That earned him a lazy smile from the man Kyle was planning on proposing to this summer.

"I love you more," Logan murmured. "How about we forget we have kids for five minutes?"

As if Kyle could. "Even if he was a great guy...he's sixteen. Lani's only fourteen. She's too young."

"Agreed." Logan yanked the covers over them and cuddled

close, his eyelids drooping. "How long do we have until dinner?"

Kyle checked the alarm clock on the nightstand. "Half an hour." He yawned and lowered his head to the pillow again. "You're gonna be all diplomatic and say we should give Jax a chance to prove himself, aren't you?"

Logan chuckled warmly and let his lips linger along Kyle's hairline. "Sounds to me like you came up with that diplomacy all on your own."

"Screw that," Kyle muttered. "You know, it's not too late for us to move to Florida."

"Oh sweetheart, you'd be miserable there," Logan laughed softly. "Hell, so would I at this point. And don't you think there're Jaxes in Florida?"

Kyle sighed and tried to relax.

Was this the price of loving his family? Going gray? At least his gnome wasn't itching to run off with someone in a leather jacket who smoked cigarettes and gave their foster parents grief.

"Do you miss the city life?" Kyle asked, wanting to get his mind off things.

"No. Why?"

Kyle was relieved. He worried about it sometimes—that Logan would get sick of the bush life and wanna return to comfort and more civilization.

Logan gently bumped their foreheads together, and Kyle opened his eyes. "If I wanted to move to Anchorage or somethin', would you have gone with me?"

"Of-fucking-course I would." Kyle frowned. "I might even learn how to hunt them gayders if you wanna spend more time in Flaahrida."

Logan snickered. "All right, leave the accent to actual southerners." His eyes were full of amusement. "Anyway, that's good enough for me. But I don't want to move. I love Pinnuaq, I love it up here, and I love you and the kids."

Kyle finally relaxed, and he was surer than ever that he'd pop the question to Logan this season. The guy better say yes.

*

With the staff house full of people, they ate in shifts. Kyle arrived with his family and sat down to eat with Declan, Quinn, Patrick, Nina, Caleb, and that fucking Jax.

"Last of the meat from the storage," Patrick declared, sitting down at the head of the table. "Dig in, everyone. It's good to have you home."

Kyle chugged his first glass of milk in one go and then sat back with a satisfied sigh. "We'll fill up that cache in no time, Patrick. Don't worry." He plated himself a couple moose burgers. "I see you've finally learned how to use the grinder Logan and I gave you."

"No, but I did," Nina said with a cheeky grin. "Jax helped me."

Kyle slid his gaze over to Jax, who was keeping his head down as he ate.

Kyle felt Logan's hand on his thigh, a silent acknowledgment.

"Boss?" One of the wildlife guides poked his head in the kitchen, and Patrick looked up in question. "Bill radioed in from the dock. The school class from Fairbanks is back from fishing, and they're kinda trapped in the activity center."

"Why?" Patrick lifted a brow.

The man smiled wryly. "There's a pack of wolves on the beach. The kids are refusing to go outside."

Kyle didn't see the big deal. "Are they rabid or something?" Otherwise, wolves didn't fucking attack. People needed to get that through their thick skulls.

"No, they're just close enough, and Bill's the only one on staff there," the guy said. "He's not worried, but he can't keep fifteen city kids and their two teachers from freaking out."

Patrick snorted and looked to Logan and Kyle.

Logan nodded and wiped his mouth. "We're on it."

Goddammit, Kyle was starving.

"Can I come, Dad?" Justin asked Kyle with a hopeful expression.

"Not this time, cub." Kyle stood up and poured another glass of milk. "We'll be back soon. You stay with your uncles." He guzzled the milk and then moved toward the hallway.

"You can bake a cake with me and Caleb," Nina said.

Justin was happy again.

"What about me?" Lani asked. "Can I go with you?"

Kyle turned and saw it was Logan she'd asked, and Kyle couldn't help but smile when Logan nodded and said "Sure" as if it was no big deal. It *wasn't* a big deal, yet it showed how far Logan had come.

"Wait, what?" Jax broke through his don't-give-a-fuck attitude and looked upset. "Lani can't go. It's not safe."

"I feel like we've been here before," Quinn mused, grinning at Logan.

Logan chuckled. "Let's not talk about it."

"I'll be perfectly safe," Lani told Jax with a sweet smile.

"I don't like it, baby," Jax said quietly.

Baby?

Everyone had obviously heard that, and the majority were surprised. Logan was irritated, Kyle was seething, and Jax appeared to just notice what he'd said. Anger and embarrassment colored his cheeks, which he soon covered with a blank mask.

Kyle glared and stalked over to Jax, bending down to the kid's level. "Let's get one thing straight. Lani's our daughter, yeah? *Our* baby girl—mine and Logan's. Not yours. You fuckin' got that?"

"*Dad,*" Lani gritted out. "You're humiliating me."

"We can talk about this later, people," Patrick said mildly. "Logan, Kyle, do you mind if Jax goes with you? It might be easier for him if he sees for himself that Lani's very capable of taking care of herself out there."

*

Kyle hung his rifle on his back and handed Logan his own. Four ATVs waited behind the main house, but Logan told Lani to ride behind him on his. *Good.* Easier to keep an eye on her and Jax that way.

Passing a few Retreat guests along the way, Kyle took the lead as they drove toward the ocean. He took a shortcut that brought them off the path and across a sliver of the Preserve where the terrain was a bit rockier along the shrubby landscape. Why? He wanted to see if Jax could handle it.

Unfortunately, the kid could.

Kyle flew over a hill and landed smoothly, the ocean coming into view up ahead. So did the two buildings they'd restored three years ago, and he could see the schoolkids from Fairbanks looking out the windows.

They parked right outside the activity center, and Kyle and Logan met up with Bill.

"They're down there." Bill pointed toward the rocky beach. "I'm guessing there's a dead animal nearby since the wolves are sticking around." He rolled his eyes at the kids with their faces stuck to the windows inside. "Let me know if you need help. I'll be in there, trying not to kill myself."

Kyle ignored the rifle on his back because, at the sight of four young wolves sniffing around the rocks, he knew it wasn't gonna be necessary. "Lani," he called, looking over his shoulder.

He interrupted Lani and Jax's game of shooting each other not-so-subtle glances, and she walked over to Kyle.

"You're up." Kyle took out his pistol from his holster and held it out for her. "Logan will go with you."

Logan's mouth tugged up, and he flicked his gaze between Jax and Kyle. He probably knew Kyle wanted a minute alone with Jax.

"Come here, darlin'." Logan placed a hand on Lani's shoulder, and the two walked down along the beach.

"You—get over here." Kyle jerked his chin at Jax.

Jax's jaw ticked, and his dark blue eyes flashed with defiance. At least he complied. He stuck his hands down in the pockets of his jeans and shuffled closer.

"She's too young for you," Kyle told him bluntly. "If you've really gotten your shit together, feel free to be her friend. Logan and I draw the line there."

A shot went off, and they looked over where Lani had fired a warning shot in the sky. The wolves scattered, and Logan closed in to see if there was a carcass that was luring in predators.

Kyle faced Jax again with an expectant stare.

"I get it," Jax said irritably. "Chill, for fuck's sake. I'm only…protective of her."

Yeah, and pigs could fly.

"Good talk." Kyle gave him a quick, sarcastic smile. "As you can see, our daughter doesn't need your protection, so you can back off."

Jax didn't reply. He only gazed out over the beach where Lani and Logan were looking for whatever had kept the wolves there. The wolves were long gone.

*

That night, Kyle and Logan sat on their porch with Declan and Quinn. They were just shooting the shit, having a few beers—well, Kyle was drinking a Coke—and Justin had crashed after a long day with Nina and Caleb.

"This place looks bigger when it's not covered in four feet of snow," Logan mused.

Quinn smacked his own arm. "More space for the mosquitoes."

Declan smirked and passed the spray bottle of repellent to his husband.

The sun was about to set, and Kyle checked the time. Almost midnight. The days were growing longer.

The peace was disturbed by a furious teenager running toward the cabins.

"Someone's on the warpath," Declan murmured.

Kyle and Logan sat up straighter in their Adirondack chairs as Lani approached.

"You *suck*, Dad," she spat out, glaring at Kyle. "You told Jax to stay away from me?"

"You don't talk to us like that, Ilannaq," Logan warned quietly. "Choose your next words wisely."

Kyle met Lani's stare, not intimidated for shit.

Lani shrieked and stomped her foot. A huff escaped her next, and she climbed the steps and then scowled while opening the door to their cabin.

"Just know one thing," she said. Her smile was anything but

sweet. "Where there's a will, there's a way." With that said, she went inside and slammed the door shut.

The men were silent for a while, and then Logan cleared his throat. "This summer's gonna be long, isn't it?"

Kyle sighed. "Not long enough unless it lasts until that girl's eighteen."

"Okay, so here's to a long summer." Declan held up his beer. "A long summer and a girl who has two fathers and countless uncles to keep her miserable."

"I'll toast to that," Kyle chuckled.

Logan grinned and covered Kyle's hand with his own. "Me, too. Cheers."

FOR MORE, VISIT
www.caradeewrites.com
CARA ON SOCIAL MEDIA

f FACEBOOK.COM/CARADEEWRITES

🐦 @CARADEEWRITES

📷 @CARAWRITES

Made in the USA
Columbia, SC
02 May 2017